ENDORSEMENTS

"God is at work softening the heart of embittered Kate. See how he uses life and death situations to draw her attention to him. Action packed, yet heart-warming." ~E. L.

"Katy's (Kate's) Journey of Faith tells of one woman's realization that God can take a mess and turn it into a message. No matter what we encounter in life, God is in control and helps us during our darkest times, even if we don't feel his presence. John D. Strong writes an uplifting, hopeful novel that explores what most Christians experience as they walk through the trials and tribulations of living in a fallen world." ~D. H.

"In reading John D. Strong's *Pursuit*, I found myself relating to various aspects of the main character, Kate. While I haven't gone through some of the traumatic events Kate went through, I certainly have dealt with my own traumas. Coming to terms with those events is probably one of the hardest things as humans we deal with. That is what Kate is trying to do in *Pursuit*.

"This story draws you in with conversations between Kate and her counselor as well as the recounting of things from her past that led up to her present situation. The dialogue was so rich in many places that I found myself completely engrossed in the story, and the ending certainly was a surprise! Would recommend it!" ~S. M.

Kate's Journey of Faith
Book 1

PURSUIT

John D. Strong

Cover and Interior Design: Rachel Trautmiller (inflection-studios.com)

Editor: Lora Doncea (EditsbyLora.com)

Find out more about John at https://JohnDStrong.com

ISBN-13: 979-8-9887215-0-5 (paperback)

DEDICATION

To my wife, Emma, who loves to read, but leaves the story writing to me. She says sitting in front of a computer all day would be too much to bear. Emma has taken on tasks that have freed me to work on this book, as well as given me time to write. Thank you for all your help, Love!

ONE

KATE Edwards tried to scream, but no sound came out. She was frozen with terror. The man's face was close, his evil grin leering at her, his intent clear with the *ziiiiiipping* sound. He kissed her firmly. She tried to yank her head away, but he gripped her hair and pinned her body so tightly she couldn't fight back. Panic flooded her veins as she struggled against his assault.

Then his face disappeared and the other terror charged at her. The raging beast opened its mouth. Kate felt its hot breath and smelled its putrid stench. It engulfed her head, and she tried to push against the oozing sides, choking and flailing. She screamed again, but the sound was muffled inside its gigantic mouth.

She woke with a start. Clutching the bed-sheets, she tried to breathe and slow her pounding heart. She'd suffered these same horrible nightmares for years. This one was so vivid that she relived the horrors all over again. Would she ever be free from the torment of her past?

She did everything possible to eliminate the memories. She had moved more than a thousand miles away. Then she worked herself to exhaustion to forget, hoping against hope her next sleep would be an escape.

She thought she had achieved a measure of success in separating herself from the past. Lately, she had even managed to have a few restful nights. She told herself she was finally over the worst of the night terrors.

The trigger, of course, had been receiving the envelope from him. It brought her nightmares back with a vengeance, destroying her carefully constructed, hard-fought-for defenses. All her progress eclipsed by a scrap of paper.

Why had he written? Couldn't he have just left it alone? To forget the events, she had chosen to forget *him*. This was a grave injustice, but it was necessary for her mental health. He hadn't tried contacting her for years, so why now? She opened the envelope and saw it was a letter, but shoved it back in quickly, attempting to avoid an emotional meltdown.

She had gone to many therapists over the years, trying to eliminate the nightmares. She thought therapy had finally succeeded. Obviously not.

With trembling fingers, she reached for her phone. As her hand moved, it brushed the clammy sheets. Surprised, she felt her pajamas—they were soaked as well. She knew she could not bear another episode like last night's.

She had an appointment with her therapist, Helen, that very day. What should have been a comfort was not. Helen was a nice-enough person, but Kate could not bring herself to bare her heart to this woman. She tugged her phone from her purse and called Helen, hoping for the answering service.

Helen answered. "Hello?"

Despite her still-shaking body, she chose to use her upbeat voice. "Hi, Helen. Uh, about our appointment today. I'm cancelling. And I won't be back. It's not working. Nothing personal."

"You need to give it time. Give *us* time."

"No, Helen, I'm done."

There was silence for a few seconds. "As you wish, Kate. I'm here for you in case you change your mind."

Helen was the last in a long line of therapists—hired, then discarded. Kate never found anyone who could help her find peace and resolution. She was still anxious, driven, always on edge, wary. Trusting people was out of the question, even those who deserved it.

She could not delve into her past. What was past was just that—past, wasn't it? Therapists always wanted her to go there. She wasn't going to. Too many bad memories. Awful, horrific memories.

But—would she ever find peace if she *didn't* face the past? Still shaking from her nighttime ordeal, she determined to face her terrors. It was time to quit running. She would read the dreaded letter. She picked it up, but horror flooded her instantly. "No! No! No!"

She thrust the letter from her. She glanced at the picture on her dresser, lying facedown. Why did he have to contact her? She wanted to live her life, and he could enjoy his. They were worlds apart, yet still connected by love and history that intertwined them. There was no separating the bond they shared, one forged in her childhood. She couldn't forget him, no matter how hard she tried.

All her attempts to seal off the past failed when she received one unread letter. The memories flooded in. She could no longer shut them out, not that she ever could, but now they were overwhelming her. She feared she was having a breakdown.

She whipped out her phone, opened her contacts to Helen's number, then stopped. How could she tell that woman? There was no way she could understand. But she couldn't hold it all in any longer, so she needed to find someone to help her before she snapped.

Hands trembling, she looked up therapists, psychiatrists, psychologists—degrees or levels of skill didn't matter. Leonard Baer was the first name she saw. What could it hurt to check out a new therapist? If she didn't like him, she could refuse to go back. It wasn't like she'd never done that before. She called before she could talk herself out of it.

Dr. Baer had an open appointment in two days and she grabbed it. Her department would just have to keep it together in her absence, no small feat.

As she got ready for work, she thought of all the problems that awaited her. That would help her avoid thinking about her nightmares. Supervising the supposed professionals in her department should not require so much checking up on, reminding, and sending sharply worded emails about missed deadlines. She even put the finishing touches on her team's work, doing what *they* should be doing. She had to keep up with more and more demands from the marketing department.

It was a wonder that Hanson & Son could still compete in increasingly tighter markets, given the difficulty Kate experienced in getting her department to meet the high standards set by Hiram Hanson IV. She had to smile a bit—whoever would have named their baby Hiram? And then repeated it three more times?

Nonetheless, she would have to make changes in her department. She and her staff produced all the material, hard copy as well as online advertising, for the entire company. The problem was that her staff of creative individuals thought their best work only happened when they were "on" or their creative juices were flowing or whatever.

She didn't understand that. She needed her creative geniuses, but she needed them to meet deadlines. Motivating them was becoming harder, while the deadlines and workload were increasing. Too often she had had to finish what her staff had left uncompleted.

It didn't help that Hiram the fifth was hired for her department, rather than the very talented recent applicant. She'd desperately wanted him, but it didn't matter—Hiram V was hired in his place. There was no budget for more staff, she was told, and she was not at liberty to let people go without immense hassle from HR and Hiram IV himself. Hiram IV believed in giving employees multiple chances, far more than they deserved. Kate scowled and shook her head.

Four, as Hiram IV was known to his employees—not necessarily to his face, although he undoubtedly knew—was not so understanding toward his managers. They had to get the work done according to schedule.

It was an odd combination, this understanding of the workers but not the managers. It contributed to a greater-than-normal turnover of managers who were stuck with the previous manager's "problems."

She was beginning to understand how and why she had been hired for such a responsible position with her limited experience in the field. She had been hired after only a couple short stints in previous companies. She did graphic design in one, and was an assistant manager in the last one.

When she'd been hired, she thought it was her education, GPA, and especially her great portfolio, in addition to the experience she did have. Now, however, it seemed she had been hired to give the previous manager an "out" or to fill a spot that needed a warm body. Perhaps that was a cynical viewpoint, but it had merit given the situation in which she now found herself. Of course, her outlook was perhaps adversely influenced by her state of frustration, fatigue, and nightmares.

How many quality people had left Hanson & Son was beyond Kate's knowing, but she was beginning to understand why they had left. She loved her job, churning out snappy brochures, flyers, and eye-catching advertising. The marketing manager had complimented her on more than one occasion, and he was not one to give out many compliments.

Five, as she had begun to refer to Hiram V, was a drag on her department. Granted, he did have to learn, but he wasn't up to the caliber she needed. The retired employee he replaced was one of her star creators, who also shared her belief in quality work on time.

Maybe all she needed was some time off. Her accrued vacation time was enviable, though her position of "babysitter" was not conducive to using it. What would happen to her department in her absence? What *could* happen might take her months to correct, all while keeping up with the marketing department's demands for more and more, better and better, faster and faster.

It was getting to her. She always tried to run at peak efficiency and productivity, so one might imagine her difficulty in answering the twice-yearly questions. How have you improved over the last six months? What can you do to improve your work and that of your employees? How can you make your department more efficient? On and on.

She didn't need them looking over her shoulder, looking for ways to improve—she did that herself, always alert for efficiency, coupled with the quality expected and demanded. She did it, so she didn't require, nor want, their meddling. She knew what needed doing and how to get it done.

***

"So," Dr. Baer said as Kate sat in his office, "I read your information last evening. I'm the eighth in a long line of therapists, the last several here in the area. So why keep changing?"

"Is that a crime?"

"No. It is, however, indicative that you're in conflict within. You want to talk, but you don't want to talk."

Same as Helen. "You sound as though you think I'm crazy."

"No, severely conflicted, but definitely not crazy. You faced something too painful to speak of plainly. Instead, you beat around the bush, but never come to the point of admitting that what happened,

happened. But now it has become too overwhelming to keep it shut in.

"It's often when the pain of remaining the same becomes greater than the pain of looking into past events that substantive change occurs in a person's life. My guess is that is where you are."

The man said his piece, then just sat quietly, looking at her. However, he had a more compassionate look on his countenance than the others. As he waited, the silence grew deafening. Apparently he wasn't going to talk, so she had to say *something*.

"Dr. Baer, I ... I don't know where to start. I was okay until I got the letter."

"I doubt that."

She glared at him. "What do you mean? How do you know?"

He shrugged and put his hands out in front of him. "Trouble doesn't come from a letter, generally, but rather from what the letter *represents*. But I don't know. I was only guessing.

"I'd also like to know—are you willing to go through what it's going to take to find healing? I won't sugarcoat this process. It's hard and it's painful, but very freeing once you reach the other side. I think unwillingness to face the truth has kept you jumping therapists. You want help, but you're not willing to engage the memories.

"I, for one, would like to see you free. Will you hang in there? For that greater good?"

Kate leaned forward in her chair. Her throat tightened, but she managed a whisper. "Are you going to bail on me if I don't?"

Deep within, she knew changing therapists was her way to avoid memories. The problem was, her attempt at avoidance wasn't working. So would she take the plunge and delve into the memories? Or would she continue to avoid them, trying to make them disappear?

He looked steadily into her eyes. "You haven't answered my question."

Her right foot lifted on her toes and began shaking. She licked her lips. "So does that mean you'll send me away if I don't give the right answer? I need someone I can trust who won't abandon me. It may just take some work to get where we need to get."

He smiled. It was friendly, compassionate. He reached a hand out to her, touched her hand lightly, then withdrew it. "I never abandon a client. I understand hurt and fear and reticence to open oneself up to another. I was there myself. When I started my practice, I vowed I would never abandon a hurting person.

"Some clients struggle and struggle, but never take the leap of faith and enter into their pain. I also have those who are willing to work on what bothers them. Make no illusions, Kate—getting well is hard work, on my part and yours. It's hard and painful, but on the other side, you will find peace and freedom you never had."

He smiled again. "Some people need a ton of time and reassurance to open up, so I choose to give them all they need."

She cleared her throat. "I have a good life. But I have experienced trauma, devastating trauma. Some might say it wasn't anything much, but … oh, I don't know …"

She held her head in her hands. Tears flooded her eyes.

"One person's trauma isn't the same as another's. Our hurt is just that—ours. Whether another might feel the same way about it is immaterial. What matters is *your* interpretation.

"What the events taught you about yourself, God, the world, and the way things work is what's important. What we have to deal with is our *interpretation*. We start with the events, but we have to get down to what your thoughts were and are."

Those were the exact things she was trying to erase forever.

***

She met with Dr. Baer several more times, but just could not bring herself to divulge her memories.

In one of their sessions, she fixed him with a steely gaze. "You think I'm unwilling to deal with my issues, don't you? Answer me truthfully—you think I'm not willing to do the work, don't you?"

He returned her gaze, smiling kindly. "I think you are a very hurt woman with much harm done to you. But I also think you have what it takes to honestly look at it."

Kate rubbed her clammy hands together and leaned forward. "I work to near exhaustion, hoping I can fall asleep easily and avoid nightmares. I'm on edge all the time. I snapped at my best employee today, then was snippy with the boss, the big boss. I'm afraid I'm going to end up in an asylum, besides losing my job. I'm jumpy. I don't sleep."

Kate began crying silently, arms wrapped tightly around herself.

He was silent for a few moments, then spoke softly. "Kate, I think your mind is telling you it's time. You cannot push this down any longer. Your old ways of coping aren't working."

Nodding, she stood up and wiped her eyes. "I'll call you."

She took a week of her accumulated vacation time to work on erasing the past forever. Halfway through, she knew her way wasn't going to work. The memories still stared her full in the face, demanding to be dealt with. She must share the unshareable, speak the unspeakable.

Time to face the heartache and terrors of her pushed-down, pushed-away past. She could put it off no longer. Reluctantly, she made an appointment with Dr. Baer.

Sitting in his office with her head bowed, her hands shook uncontrollably.

His kind voice broke into her thoughts. "I admire your courage, Kate. I know this is hard for you."

Courage? I have no courage. I'm scared to death.

"Kate, courage is not the absence of fear, but doing the thing that scares us, despite the fear."

She looked up. One thing about this guy—he seemed to know what she was thinking.

"I know you're terrified, so telling your story is very courageous. I feel honored that you would share it with me."

She crossed her arms, wondering if his last statement was mocking her. Helen, as well as some other of her therapists had put her down. At least it felt that way.

"It is *always* an honor to share a person's pain and to walk with her through it." Again, he seemed to be one jump ahead of her.

She saw the compassion on his face and heard it in his words. She placed her hand on her shaking knee. With tears in her eyes, a tissue already in hand, she spoke barely above a whisper. "I don't know where to begin."

"Start anywhere."

She cleared her throat, beads of sweat on her forehead. "I was an only child. My parents showered me with material things. Life was good. My father had a good job, so we didn't have to do without. My mother was a homemaker. We had nice vacations. My parents got along—I was never aware of any problems between them."

Her voice caught. "Then ... I'm sorry. I don't think I can go on."

"I know it scares you, but we're on the verge of something important. Please continue."

She clutched her hands together. "If I start, I may never stop, Dr. Baer. Please don't make me go on."

He shook his head, smiling. "I never *make* someone do something. I only encourage them to share what has them tied up in knots. I think *you* want to continue."

She nodded, and took a deep breath. "It was about time for my eleventh birthday. A gala event was planned. Friends from school and a few neighbors were invited. I was giddy with excitement—my parents told me they had a big surprise present I would love. They had to travel a ways to get whatever it was." She stopped as her throat choked up.

"The suspense is killing me. What was it?"

She shook her head. A tear dripped off her nose. "I don't know. I'll never know. On the way home, a semi crossed the median and destroyed their car, killing them instantly. I went from a pampered little girl to an orphan in an instant."

She shifted in her chair and blotted her eyes. "The next few days are a blur. Relatives and friends took care of the funeral arrangements and me for a few days, but when it was all over, no one wanted me. This aunt couldn't because her house was too small. Another had too many kids of her own. I overheard the discussions when they thought I was asleep. Nobody wanted me."

She stared at the floor for several moments, then looked up with a wet face. "I went from being a very loved and cared-for little girl to someone no one wanted.

"I was finally pawned off on poor old Uncle Ned. He was, and still is, I imagine, an old bachelor. The others guilted him into taking me. I left all my friends, my home, and moved into this dingy old cabin in the woods of Montana. I had to be driven twenty miles to town for school, to shop, to do anything, even see friends, of which there were very few anyway."

He leaned back in his chair. "Uncle Ned sent you the letter."

"Yeah. Don't get me wrong. He became very dear to my heart—he loved me as if I were his own. I love him with my whole being. I haven't had contact with him for years."

He leaned forward with his head cocked. "Okay, hold on. Something here isn't making sense. You love him, yet you hated receiving a letter from him. You say you love him, yet you have had no contact for years. Help me out here."

"Haven't I told you enough for one session?"

He hesitated before speaking, then smiled. "Sure, enough for today. What you have told me is terribly sad and traumatic beyond imagination. I did not mean to downplay it. I just don't understand the disconnect between loving your uncle and having no contact with him. That makes no sense to me. There's more to this."

"Another time—I'll try."

A few days later, after a difficult day at work, Kate sat with Dr. Baer. She smiled lamely. "A couple nights ago, I woke from a nightmare screaming. I woke the neighbors, who rushed to my door to make sure I wasn't being murdered. I made what excuses I could, then I resolved not to sleep until I saw you.

"I didn't make it, of course, but I was so exhausted when I finally did sleep that I didn't wake the neighbors again. Will I ever be free of these horrors? I can't go on living like this."

His brow was furrowed and his eyes bore into hers. "Are you thinking of ending your life, Kate? I didn't think so, but this is the first time I've heard you talk like this."

She shook her head. "No, but I have to do something."

"Just please stay with it, with us," he urged, his hand held out. "I believe you will find peace if you bring your past out into the open, keep facing it instead of continuing to live in denial. Please go on with your story. You went to live with Uncle Ned."

She pulled in a deep breath. "I had been traumatized by my parents' untimely death, then my relatives' refusal to take me, and then having to go live with Uncle Ned way out in Montana. He lived out in the woods, almost as a hermit. He hunted and trapped for food and some income. He appeared to be below the poverty line, although I never lacked for what I needed. He had withdrawn from society.

"I know, Dr. Baer. It looks like I don't care for the old man. I do, but the memories … I just can't …" she said, her voice trailing off.

"So you go from life of the party to being a hermitess?" he said. "A difficult transition, but not enough to bring about nightmares, is it? Kate, I'm not minimizing what happened to you—it was awful, but I don't understand the nightmares. Again, I am not downplaying the horror of losing your folks, but is that where these nightmares are from? I think there might be more to this story."

Kate wrung her hands for a few moments, then opened her mouth. "For years, I thought I could keep most of the memories at bay. It took great effort, but I could sometimes tone them down. But hard as I try to push them away, they crash into me now with a ferocity that terrifies me. I fear I am losing … my mind."

"Please—"

"The faces, the two faces—they meld together into my dreams, now even into my waking thoughts. I'm terrified of sleep, even of being awake. I drive myself to exhaustion, hoping against hope that I will sleep without seeing them."

Her forehead glistened with sweat. "Hang on, Dr. Baer, we're headed into deep waters. The faces …"

She stepped to the edge of the precipice, looked over into the yawning abyss. She hesitated, but knew she was going over. She was the little girl again, back in the Montana cabin, back with Uncle Ned.

TWO

WHEN Kate arrived in Pickerel, Montana, Uncle Ned was waiting for her at the bus station. The driver retrieved her suitcases and plopped them on the sidewalk. Uncle Ned had a beat-up old pickup, which was a far cry from the shiny new car she'd ridden in with her parents. After surveying the dingy and messy cab, she brushed a couple pieces of paper off her seat, then gingerly climbed in.

The man looked her over, then spoke gruffly. "Sorry about your mother. She was my sister, although she would not have admitted it. Well, water over the dam. We gotta get on with life now."

Uncle Ned did not say much more about her parents. Over time, Kate pieced together from snippets of comments that there had been some sort of conflict between brother and sister that had never been resolved. She also discovered her uncle held grudges as fiercely as a tight-fisted old miser held on to his gold. He wouldn't, or couldn't, let them go.

Uncle Ned almost never brought up the subject of her parents after the first few days, but also did not scold her for mentioning them. He listened and nodded like he cared about her feelings.

She remembered the first time she saw the cabin. It was in a clearing in the woods, smoke curling up from the chimney. It was not run down, but it would never have met her father's approval. The inside would not meet her mother's standards of neatness or cleanliness either. She hoped that he at least had indoor plumbing. She stood there with her mouth open, gaping at her new home, unable to move.

Uncle Ned looked at her. "Yeah, it ain't much, kid, but it's home. I hope you'll get to like it."

Kate set her suitcases down, wondering if she had a room. At home she had had her own room, her own playroom, and another room just for her.

Her uncle looked at her. "I got no bedroom here, so you don't either. My bed's over there."

He pointed at a messy unmade bed in the corner. "I guess you can sleep on, well, let's see. Um, well, I guess you can take my bed, and I'll sleep on the floor."

Kate wrinkled up her nose at an unpleasant odor. Whether it came from the bed or her uncle, she couldn't tell. Walking to the bed, she discovered the sheets on his bed didn't look or smell like her beautiful clean white sheets at home.

She turned her head away from the unpleasant odor. "That's okay, Uncle. I can sleep on the floor."

He handed her a blanket. "Suit yourself. Best get ready for bed. Tomorrow, we got work to do."

"Work?"

"Yeah, gotta clean up the place now we got a female livin' here. I'll need some help with the cleaning. I guess that'll be where you come in."

She looked at him in surprise. They'd had a maid who did all their cleaning and a cook for meal preparation. She'd never had to lift a finger, nor had her parents, as long as she could remember in her old home. *Her* home—gone, sold to someone else. Now she was lost in the vast wildness of Montana. And they didn't even live in the town, but a long, long ways outside of it. There were woods all around and no other houses—no cars, no malls, just nothing, and lots of it.

She hadn't known that such places existed. Maybe she'd read of them, but they hadn't seemed like real places, just stories.

It was a shock to Kate that some people didn't have workers to do the cleaning and cooking. She had sort of realized some of her friends might not have had the number of workers that she had, but the fact that people actually lived in homes where *they* did all the work was beyond her understanding.

She looked around for some means of privacy, but she saw nothing. Was her uncle going to undress in front of her? Was she to do the same in front of him?

She needn't have worried about him. He took off his shirt and climbed into bed, pants and all.

She waited until her uncle was snoring loudly, then undressed and put on her pajamas. She would have liked to use the bathroom, but was afraid it was outside. She'd heard relatives whispering about her uncle's terrible living conditions. But they still made her live with him.

Despite her grief and shock at her new surroundings, she did manage to fall asleep. It was a short night—she was still deeply asleep when someone called her. She sat up, sleepy, rubbing her eyes.

She looked around. Something was definitely wrong. Her TV was gone, her soft bed was hard, and her plush pillow was nowhere to be found.

"Where am I?" she asked, frightened.

Suddenly, a man's hand touched her shoulder. She pulled away. Her father had rarely touched her. Besides, the hand was too rough to belong to her father. Who was this man?

A gentle voice spoke. "Katy, it's Uncle Ned, remember? You came to live with me here in Montana. Your folks …"

She didn't want to remember, but she did. Her parents were dead and her relatives shipped her off to live in the wilderness with a man she didn't know.

"I know, Uncle … Ned. Where's the TV? The news was always on at home."

Uncle Ned smiled faintly. "Katy, out here, life is different. Not as much fancy stuff, more just getting by. Survival is the name of the game, especially winter, and when winter's over, we get ready for the next one."

Uncle Ned gently put his hand on her shoulder again. She wasn't used to a man touching her. Her mother had hugged her some, but her father didn't show her physical affection. She tensed, and his hand fell from her shoulder.

In time, she came to realize one of the ways her uncle showed her affection was by touch, and she began to allow it. Gradually, although it took a long time, she even allowed him to hug her. Her favorite show of affection from him was his gentle kiss on top of her head.

As she stood up that first day in her pajamas, she wondered where she could get dressed in privacy. She looked around the one-room cabin.

"Oh," he finally said. "Follow me." He led the way to the bathroom. "You may dress in here. I will, too."

He explained "running water" meant that water ran *out* of the house, but the toilet tank had to be hand filled by carrying buckets from the kitchen which had a hand pump to bring water from the well. Hand washing after using the bathroom was done in the kitchen. Water for the bathtub was carried from the kitchen, after being heated on the woodstove. She was welcome to have a bath as often as she liked, but she would have to heat and carry her own water.

She dressed and relieved her screaming bladder. She then reappeared, and came out into the kitchen where he was preparing breakfast.

"Katy, I know this is hard for you, losin' your mom and dad and your home, but give it time. You'll get into this way of life, if you let yourself. Get involved. Live life in the fresh air, learn to love, as well as respect, the wilderness.

"Never had kids." He looked directly into her eyes. "I will treat you as my own. Life is real different here, but it's free, the air is clean and fresh, but you gotta work at it. You can be happy or miserable, but it'll go lots easier if you choose to be happy."

"How can I be happy?" she snapped, feeling anger burning in her heart. She instantly cringed. The one time she remembered lashing out at her mother, she was shut down immediately, and sent to her room. "I'm sorry, Uncle."

" 'Course you're angry, Katy. It ain't fair to lose your folks, then be sent off to this faraway place with an old coot. 'Course you gotta grieve your loss—all sorts, not just your parents, but your friends, being waited on hand and foot, your school, fancy vacations.

"Not makin' light of your problems, Katy, but other people lost things too. Your mom and me, we lost our mom. It was a terrible loss, but an older friend told me I could choose to be happy or be miserable. I chose happy. Yes, I grieved, and even now there is a hole in my heart, but I choose to live happy. It is a choice only we can make."

"How come you don't have a family, Uncle Ned?" Her mom called that being nosy, but she wanted to know.

"Had a girl once," he answered with a faraway look in his eyes. "She would have loved it out here. We were in school together. My mom said it was 'puppy love.' I know you don't know what that means, Katy, but it's just a grown-up way of telling kids they're too young to understand love and marriage for life. But I knew I was gonna marry that girl. I was crazy about her."

"So what happened?"

His face grew sad, and she sensed that he had had losses too.

"She and a friend went canoeing. They were swept over the dam, crashing into the rocks below. The fire department found her friend that same day, but her body was not found until a few days afterward, farther downriver."

"What was her name?"

Uncle Ned smiled. "Katy."

"That's what you call me."

"Yeah. You remind me of her—spirited, curious, kind. You don't mind me calling you that, do you?"

"It's okay—I kinda like it."

***

"And he still calls me that, Dr. Baer," Kate said. "I've always been Katy to him, although I go by Kate now. The way he said it made me feel special, even more so than I did with my parents.

"I didn't realize it then, but over time I understood his love, and that he gave it generously. My parents met my physical needs—Uncle Ned fed my emotional needs too. He went above and beyond what my parents did, giving me time, attention, himself."

"Well, Kate, I feel we are making progress. With all the trauma you have described, despite the love you felt from your uncle, it is small wonder you have nightmares. Don't you feel that talking about this is helping?"

Kate stared at him, then scowled, crossing her arms. "Dr. Baer, you have no idea of the trauma I endured. What I have told you so far is nothing."

"Oh. Well, how about next time we get into that?"

"If you are to understand, you must get the whole picture. And to do that, I have to tell the entire story, not a piece here and a piece there. It will take a lot of time, but if you're worried about being paid, I have a generous package that covers plenty of mental health services."

"Farthest thing from my mind. I was thinking about relief from the thoughts that are torturing you."

***

At her next session with Dr. Baer, Kate was not as anxious. Maybe she was starting to trust him.

She picked up where she left off, explaining what it felt like when she was a little girl.

She didn't think she would ever get used to having to carry water to use the toilet. Getting dressed in the narrow bathroom was difficult and uncomfortable. Sleeping in the same room as someone else, especially a man, made her anxious.

On her fifth day at her new home, Uncle Ned called her early, way earlier than she was used to. "Katy, time to rise and shine. Today's cleaning day— *and* wash day."

She moved more quickly than she would have at home to get up, dress, and use the bathroom. She was afraid dawdling wouldn't be tolerated.

She soon reappeared, dressed and hungry. She sat at her place at the small table. Breakfast was typically eggs and bacon. Gone were the days of fruity sweet cereals that she loved, or the gourmet meals that Mildred, their cook, whipped up. Uncle Ned's cooking was at best "tolerable," a word she applied to many situations. "Tolerable" described something not great, but not terrible either. You could get by if something was "tolerable."

Over the years, she had many "tolerable" meals with Uncle Ned, not as delicious as she was used to, but they filled her stomach and gave her energy to do work.

She wondered what she would do for fun, but found out right away there was very little playtime. Uncle Ned would always say, "You may as well have fun workin', 'cause either way, the work's gotta get done, so you may as well have fun doin' it."

She had to learn how to wash dishes, but first she had to learn how to pump the water with the hand pump, then heat the water on the wood stove. It was far more tedious than the kind of life normal people lived, but that was life here in the cabin. It took her many weeks, but she eventually became an expert at heating water on the woodstove for kitchen use and bathroom needs. At least, waste water ran outside to a septic system. It shocked her that people actually lived this way. Maybe in far-off places they did, but not here in America.

She was slowly getting used to the lack of modern conveniences, even though she missed them terribly her first months. Thankfully, laundry was taken into town and done at the laundromat. Still, it was time-consuming.

At first, she felt as if she had fallen into a Cinderella-like existence, slaving away at tons of work. In her first few days with Uncle Ned, she imagined herself swept away by a handsome prince to live in his palace with servants doing all the work.

Whining had never worked with her parents. Although they spoiled her, they did not tolerate whining or complaining. Her uncle didn't look like the kind of person who would either. She kept her complaints to herself. Besides, she didn't really have time to whine about all the work.

He showed her how to handle the kitchen clean-up. He also taught her how to feed the woodstove and keep the fire going in the cold months, which were a good part of the year. At least he didn't just give her work to do and sit around watching her work. No, he worked as well, often longer, and as she came to realize eventually, harder.

In time, she came to handle the inside work, and made the cabin more of a home with her feminine touch. She cleaned, more often and quite more thoroughly than he had. The place certainly smelled and looked a whole lot better.

She hoped he wouldn't be angry that she wanted to clean up the cabin, including picking up his clothes when he left them on the floor or bed. Eventually he even began to fold his clothes over the chair and only rarely did he leave socks or clothes out of place.

After she'd been with him for a couple weeks, he went to town. He left her with a list of instructions. His last was delivered most sternly. "Do *not* go outside. Katy, it is very important that you do not go out of the cabin. In time you will know why, but for now, you must obey."

She looked at his face—serious, stern, even. She nodded, every fiber of her being poised to obey. Even if she had wanted to disobey, she wouldn't dare.

She felt very alone with no one there. There was not even any way to contact someone. What if something happened to him? Did anyone even know she was out here?

To her immense relief, he *finally* returned. He placed supplies on the kitchen table. "There's more."

She watched out the window. He retrieved a wagon out of the woodshed. On his return from the truck, he had large containers in the wagon.

When he came back in, she asked, "What's in those big things in the wagon?"

"They hold gas for the generator which produces our electricity for lights and the refrigerator."

He went back out for a few moments, returning with a bunch of sticks in his arms.

"What are the sticks for?" she asked. "For the stove?"

"No, these are for pine knot torches. I use them when I'm outside splitting wood, especially at night," he replied. "They give off light, but also are helpful to keep wild animals away, since animals fear fire."

Her brow furrowed. "Oh."

During dinner, he said, "Well, I ran into George Wadhams today."

"Who?"

"The school truant officer. He makes sure all kids are going to school. He knew you were coming because I already gave the school your records from your previous school. He wondered why you hadn't been in school yet.

"I apologized for the delay, explaining that you just lost your folks and were getting adjusted to a whole new way of life, being from the city and all. He said okay, but to get you in school right away. I told him I would."

It was then Kate panicked. A new school—new kids. She had never been the new kid. Around here, it was probably a one-room schoolhouse. Mean kids and bullies were probably all around. Her mind raced with the worst possibilities.

She discovered they had a school in Pickerel, and it had several rooms in fact. She and Uncle Ned met with the principal, Mrs. Pratt, who explained what class Kate would be in, who her teacher was, and what room. She was to start the very next day.

Mrs. Pratt asked to speak with Uncle Ned privately. Kate waited on the bench outside the principal's office. Despite the closed door, she overheard him discussing with the principal how Kate would manage to get to school.

"Look, Ned, I don't know why you insist on living out in that wilderness," Mrs. Pratt argued. "That's no way for a child to live."

"Ma'am, that is my home, and you know very well 'most every child in your school, girls as well as boys, learns how to live here. They hunt and trap and wander out in the woods, even in the dead of winter. It's our way, and just because you city folk don't understand, doesn't mean we should change to fit your idea of life."

Kate was shocked to hear her mild-mannered uncle speak so forcefully, especially to a school official. She shifted on the bench.

"Ned, I didn't mean to offend you," Mrs. Pratt said soothingly. "It's just that most of the children you speak of live in town or a bit out, not the fifty miles you do."

"Twenty, not fifty."

"In a blizzard, two miles may as well be fifty. What're you gonna do when you get snowed in? What if you have an emergency? An eleven-year-old can't drive and even if she could, she wouldn't be able to dig your truck out. You have more to think about than just yourself now."

Kate peeked through the window into the principal's office, and caught the glare her uncle gave Mrs. Pratt. She sat down quickly and hugged her arms around herself. She never wanted Uncle Ned to look at her like that.

On the way home, they stopped at the hardware store to pick up a few things.

James Harrison, the owner, said the same thing as they were paying for their purchases. "Living off the land ain't no way for a kid to live, not in these times. Ned, you're outta your mind. What're you gonna do in an emergency? No phone, no radio, nothing. How you gonna get help when you need it?"

Uncle Ned glared at him. "You mind your own business, James Harrison," he replied angrily. "My business is just that—*my* business. I'll never live in this town again, ever!" With that remark, he stomped out of the store, pulling Kate with him.

"You oughtta let that go!" Harrison called after him. Kate turned, but her uncle continued on without so much as a glance back.

The ride home was very quiet. Kate felt a little afraid, not as much from a new school with new kids, but of her uncle. He had never been unkind nor spoken harshly to her, but his attitude and sharp words in town caused her to wonder just how safe she was. They ate dinner mostly in silence. Then she went to bed early, as it seemed safer, plus, in sleep, she could forget her grief and worry.

THREE

KATE tried to sleep, but tossed and turned much of the night, thinking about her uncle's harsh words with the principal and the man in the store. She'd wanted to ask him about it, but she was afraid.

"How'd you sleep, Katy?" he asked.

"Okay, I guess," she replied, yawning. "No, not really. I couldn't sleep very well."

He smiled at her. "Normal, I guess, for someone who lost people she loves."

"It's not that. I thought you were a nice guy, and then you were cross with the principal and the man in the store."

After she spoke, she looked down at her plate. Suppose he didn't like her saying that? Suppose he got angry at *her*?

"Katy, look at me. You have nothing to fear from me. I'm not your father, but I am your legal guardian."

She looked up at him. "What's that mean?"

"It means that I act as if I were your father. I take care of you, and yes, it means I make rules you need to follow and punish you if you don't. But I will not get angry with you like I did those people in town. That's different. *They're* different."

"But how can I be sure?"

Rushing back into her mind was the time her father had been furious with her. Her mom said he was upset about something else, but he had yelled at her. She lost all privileges for a whole week. It had been a terrible experience.

"Katy, you have to trust me. In time, you will see that I mean what I say. For now, you have to trust me or be miserable with worry. I love you as my own."

"Why do you hate the people in town?"

Uncle Ned stared at her. "You have beautiful eyes, Katy. No time for stories today. It's off to school with you. We're leaving in ten minutes."

"I still want to know."

"I'll tell you over dinner."

He drove her to school, encouraging her the whole ride. "Just be friendly. Be yourself. They will like you."

At the end of the day, he was waiting for her as promised. During the ride home, she hoped he would keep his word to tell her why he lived where he did and why he hated the people in town. He didn't.

At dinner, she looked at him hopefully, and waited and waited. No longer able to contain herself, she spoke up. "Uncle Ned, you promised. You said you'd tell me why you hate the people in town."

He tried to smile at her, but failed. He did, however, begin his story. He received a sizable inheritance from his family, enough to purchase a home in Pickerel. People in town suggested he get together with a woman in town named Brenda. They thought she and Uncle Ned would make a good couple.

"Anyway, the people here told me Brenda and I were made for each other, which is just a grown-up way of saying that we'd be happy together.

"They all thought she was wonderful, even James Harrison at the hardware store, who knows me better'n anyone. She was quite pretty!" He grinned at Kate.

Kate grinned back, then the smile faded. "Did she die, too?"

"No. I decided to risk another try at love since the people in town seemed to think it would work. I wasn't sure it would, but I went ahead anyway. Oh, why am I talking about grown-up things to a kid?"

" 'Cause I want to know and I asked. Besides, I'll be a grown-up someday."

He smiled at her. "You surely will. Probably not as long as I think, either. So I made plans to marry Brenda and move into the house. I bought the house. Brenda asked to move in before we got married and get it ready for us. I added her name to the deed, which means she and I both owned it."

His face then turned angry. "That woman used me. She told the sheriff I hurt her. I could have gone to jail, but she agreed to me not going to jail if I made her the only owner. I denied hurting her, but no one in town believed me. She lied so she could steal my house and everyone believed her, even James Harrison. I've known him for many years. He was as close to a best friend as I ever had. We served in the army together and saved each other's life a time or two. We knew each other through and through, yet, when it came to this, he believed *her*.

"They say forgive and forget, but I just can't. I don't trust people and I don't like them. They take advantage of you, take all you've got, and leave you with nothing."

His eyes burned with anger and his voice was harsh. His face contorted into a horrible scowl. At least now she knew why he could not speak kindly to the people in town.

"Brenda lived in my house for a few years, then decided to return to the city. She sold my house, took the money, and left. She ruined my reputation besides taking my money. I'm sorry, Katy, but I won't live in town. Even if I would, I don't think I can earn enough for what we'd need to live there. Here, I own everything, and I can earn, grow, and hunt for what we need."

He shook his head. "That woman stole more than my home. She destroyed my reputation. I would always be looked at as someone who was abusive to a woman, although I never hurt her. Do you know how important a reputation is, Katy?"

"I don't even know what it is."

"Our reputation is what people believe about us. If we're honest with other people, then we will have a reputation for being honest. Normally, a person's reputation is based on truth, but sometimes, as in this case, our reputation can be hurt by someone lying about us. No matter how long I live, I will be thought of as someone who would hurt a woman."

"Maybe that's why they want you in town, so they can make sure you don't hurt *me*."

She quickly looked at her plate, holding her breath, afraid she'd really overstepped this time.

"Well, I never thought of that. But I ain't livin' in town, least of all, that one. Besides, where'd you get so smart, I mean, knowin' about such things?"

"We had classes in school."

"Well, I guess it's important to understand such things, but at such a young age as you, I wonder.

"Well, enough of that. Rest assured, I will not harm you, as long as you know that hard work won't hurt you." He winked at her.

She smiled shyly.

***

Dr. Baer tapped his pen on his notes. "So did the subject come up by the townspeople?"

Kate shook her head. "No, but I think the school staff took extra efforts to ensure I was well cared for. I didn't think about it then, but I remember some things I thought were odd at the time. I was sent to the nurse more than anyone else, it seemed to me. It makes me angry now that they thought of him that way. He was never abusive to me, hardly ever even raised his voice."

"I'm so glad to hear that. How did you handle all of the drastic changes in your life? I'm sure it was very difficult since you were so young."

"Yes, it was tough. Every single thing in my life changed."

"Will you tell me more?"

She sighed and nodded, going back in time in her mind.

***

The shock of Kate's new surroundings, with a whole different way of life, kept her feeling unsettled. Now that she understood her chores, she began wondering what could be done about her bedroom needs.

33

She desperately wanted her own room and privacy. She had no space to call her own.

Worse, she slept in the same room as a grown man. Although Uncle Ned never did anything inappropriate, it still felt weird and awkward.

One evening, Kate looked around to see if there were any possibilities. They could hang a rope with a blanket over it for privacy. She still would love to have her own room, but that might have to do. She glanced up at the loft. It extended over the kitchen, was piled high with stuff, and there wasn't any way to get up there. But maybe, somehow, it could be made to work.

Anyway, she would bring it up. Something *had* to be done. The most that could go wrong is he might say no, and she would be where she was now. She crossed her fingers.

At dinner that evening, she piped up. "Um, I was wondering if I could have a bedroom in the loft. I had my own room at home. I know this isn't home, but—"

"It's home now." He looked up at the loft. "Got a bunch of junk up there. Let me think on it."

Well, at least he didn't say no.

Saturday morning, she was awakened by hammering. She opened her eyes and saw Uncle Ned pounding on the wall between the main floor and the loft. She grabbed her clothes and ran into the bathroom. Whatever he was doing looked interesting, since it was out of the normal routine. By the time she returned, he had stopped banging. He was standing back as if admiring his handiwork.

It was then Kate saw what he had been creating—a ladder built into the wall. But what made it more interesting was that it was a ladder leading up to the loft. Was it possible? Was she to have her own bedroom at last?

Although very curious and not shy, she still didn't dare ask. If the answer were no, the disappointment would be crushing. He wasn't much for explaining what he was up to until it was necessary for her to know.

He must have caught the unasked question. "You know, I grew up without a mother. Never had a wife or a daughter. So havin' you here is a mite new to me. I shoulda figured you'd like your own space, but as I never had a female around before, I never gave it a thought.

"I'm glad you're up because we have lots to do today. Lots besides our normal Saturday work. I already ate so's I can work while you eat and—"

Kate turned away as hot tears sprang to her eyes, then rolled down her cheeks. Her voice quavered. "You always eat with me." She turned back to him.

He gently touched her shoulder. "I'm sorry. I didn't think it mattered."

"Well, it does." She sniffled.

"Well, then, I guess I'll have to eat another breakfast. Come along now, dry those tears. I didn't know it was important to you."

"You always eat with me. If you're going to eat early, I want you to get me up so we can eat together."

"Duly noted."

She held out her hands. "What's that mean?"

"I mean, I'll do what you asked."

She didn't know it then, but she came to learn Ned Perkins was a man of his word. It was rare that he didn't eat breakfast and dinner with her, and then only missing an occasional one for a legitimate reason.

With breakfast over, she began heating water to wash dishes. He laid his hand on her forearm.

"Let's leave the dishes. We can use them again for lunch and dinner," he said.

Unusual. He always wanted them washed after every meal. She guessed that before she came, he didn't do them as often, but whatever the reason, he was cutting her a break today.

She found out, however, that she wasn't getting off easier. The work he'd planned for her and himself was heavier, dirtier, and took most of the day. They were going to clean the loft.

The dust had obviously lain there since the beginning of time, or maybe longer. She coughed a lot as they moved items. Uncle Ned assembled the bed frame that was up there while she swept out the dresser drawers. She wiped them down with cleaner. At least the mattress and box springs had been covered with tarps, and then sheets underneath the tarps, so they were clean. Thank goodness.

There was some wood up there, long pieces that he pushed off the edge to where he could reach them from downstairs. "Katy, you finish cleaning up here. I have some woodwork to do. But first, let me do this."

He drove a large nail into one of the support posts and another one into another post near the ladder. He then grabbed a rope and tied it to both nails. He pointed to three large plastic bags.

"When you are done cleaning, open those bags. There are clean sheets for the bed and tons of blankets. Put a couple on your bed. You will need them for our cold Montana winters. Save one to hang over the rope I just hung. That will have to do for a door. It will give you privacy, and sort of your own room."

Kate squealed and grabbed him around the waist, giving him a tremendous hug. "Thank you! Thank you! I love it!" She broke free and worked with renewed energy.

While she worked in the loft, on the main level Uncle Ned sawed and hammered. He used both a large handsaw and his chainsaw, unusual since he was in the house. When curiosity overcame her, she climbed down to see what he was doing.

What she saw shocked her. He was cutting a hole in the wall of the cabin. Had he lost his mind? What was he doing?

When he broke through, what Kate saw was not the outside, but the inside of another building. "What is that? And what are you doing?"

"This is my woodshed. You've seen it from outside. This is where it connects to the cabin. I've been wanting to cut a door so I, so we, could get wood without going out into the snow. In a bad snowstorm like we sometimes get, it can be dangerous to go outside to get wood. If a person falls or gets lost and can't see, they can die just a few feet from safety."

He built a door in the hole. The door was strong, fashioned out of the thick boards he had gotten in the loft. He fastened one U-shaped metal piece to either side of the frame that held the door in place. He then dropped a thick, wide board into the two metal pieces.

He pointed to the board sitting between the two metal pieces. "See this? This board reinforces the door to make it stronger, so even if the door somehow got broken, or the latch broke, this board will hold the door shut."

"Why did you make such a thick door? And why did you put the board in those metal pieces? We never had that at home."

"To make sure we have no unwanted visitors."

She waited curiously, but he said no more.

He went outside. She followed. He opened the double doors to the large, long woodshed and showed her the door he had just created. She saw the neatly piled split wood ready for the winter. There was a lot of it—tons, she imagined.

Taking a good look around, she noticed that the outside double doors leading into the woodshed also had the same U-shaped thing on each side of the doorframe on the inside. There was another thick, wide board leaning against the wall. He sure was serious about not wanting visitors. It was no wonder, considering how people had treated him.

Despite the enormous amount of wood already in the shed, he continued to split more. She heard him hard at work on the wood after she had returned to her new bedroom to finish cleaning. Her very own space, with all the privacy she could imagine, was now hers.

After dinner, she heated the water on the woodstove and washed the dishes. When the kitchen was cleaned up, she again heated water for her bath. Her muscles ached and the hot water felt wonderful. She soaked for a bit, then got out, dried off, and dressed for bed. She was more tired than she ever remembered being, but she peeked out the door at her uncle still splitting wood by the light of his pine knot torch. Surely no wild animal would come near him with that stick blazing so brightly.

"I'm going to bed. I'm really tired."

"Good night, Katy. You did a great job today. Enjoy your bedroom."

She was too tired to enjoy her new bed. Just a few moments after her head hit the pillow, she was sound asleep.

FOUR

KATE was shocked at the amount of snow that fell the first winter, even though classmates told her it was normal. The first major storm hit on their drive home from town. It snowed hard and came down fast. She was getting used to walking the nearly hundred yards from the parking area just off the road to the cabin in the warmer weather. But she worried about what it would be like in the deep snow.

As they drove home, the snow was piling up along the edge of the road and in the woods. How would they even get into their parking area? And how in the world would they make it through the snow to the cabin? Thankfully, someone had plowed out their parking space. Uncle Ned pulled in and shut the truck off.

She could see the snow getting deeper by the minute. How would either of them make it?

The sled in the back of his pickup made sense now. Apparently, it wasn't for fun. It would be necessary to haul what they purchased in town through the deep snow.

They both loaded the sled. He looked around, smelled the air, then said, "Looks like it's gonna be a good storm. Well, we bought enough things to keep us for a while. Got plenty of fuel for the generator, food, and wood for the stove. Oh, and I bought a pair of snowshoes for you."

What were snowshoes?

"They're for walking in deep snow. Figured we'll be doing some snowshoeing back and forth from the truck to the cabin. You'll see."

They made it to the cabin just as darkness fell. Kate was exhausted from the long walk in the snow, for even though Uncle Ned had broken trail, she still struggled to walk. Now it made sense why he insisted she wear snow boots today. Her favorite sneakers which she had wanted to wear would not have kept her feet dry.

That night, she was afraid when the wind howled and snow pelted the windows and roof. She tried to sleep, but she had never been in such a storm, especially so far from any other people. What if they had a problem, she wondered. They had no phone. They were all alone. What if Uncle Ned got sick or hurt? There was no way she could get him to the truck, and even if she did, she couldn't drive it, nor dig it out of the snow.

She desperately wished she could have been back home where life wasn't scary. Things were predictable—go to school, watch TV, do homework, play, eat, watch more TV, play with one of her friends. Out here, there were no friends. In fact, besides Uncle Ned, there wasn't anybody.

The next day was Saturday—the first of two days of freedom. Freedom only meant freedom from school, not from work, as there were always things to

do. If there were no other chores to do, she was supposed to stack wood in the woodshed. But she wasn't
allowed to go in the woodshed until the outer door of
the woodshed was shut and barred. He sure was serious about preventing visitors.

After breakfast and kitchen duties, he lifted
his pair of snowshoes from the nail where they were
hung on the wall. He also retrieved her pair from a
nail beside his.

She watched, wondering how this new thing
worked. It seemed doubtful.

He smiled at her. "We are going to school today."

She frowned. "But it's Saturday."

He smiled. "There is a different school you
will be attending."

She groaned. *Another* school? It wasn't that
she disliked school, but come on, enough already.

Uncle Ned continued to smile. "Katy, relax.
You have already been attending this school."

"What? I haven't been going to another
school."

"Ah, but you have, Katy girl. You learned
how to pump water, carry it to the bathroom, wash
dishes, and feed a woodstove. Today, we are adding
an additional skill. Snowshoeing class begins now.
Watch me put my snowshoes on."

He demonstrated how to put his feet with his
boots on into the straps and then fasten the straps tight
over his boots. He undid the straps and removed his
feet from the snowshoes. "Now you do it."

Kate tried, but couldn't do it. She humphed
and sat on the floor with her arms folded.

"Do it again. First, watch me do it."

She watched intently, determined to pick it up on her second try. She tried it again. This time didn't work either.

"Here, let me show you on your snowshoes." He got her feet all strapped in.

Relieved, Kate lifted her feet, one after the other. Then she shuffled to the door.

"Whoa. Not so fast." He pulled her back from the door. "You need to do it."

He undid the straps, and insisted she strap her boots in herself.

Kate looked at him, but didn't move. Why did she have to know how to put them on? He was here.

He pointed at her. "Go on. You do it." He made her strap her booted feet in, then undo the straps and step out of the snowshoes. When she finally did it right, she looked up at him, beaming.

He grinned at her. "Very good. Now do it again."

Why? She had done it and he praised her. She hesitated.

He spoke sharply. "No, do it again, I said."

She hurried to obey, but her trembling fingers and shaking hands failed her.

He sighed, then spoke. "Oh, Katy."

Tears sprang to her eyes, and a couple began to trickle down her face. One dripped off her nose. He was disappointed in her—her gaze dropped to the floor.

Kate heard a sound beside her. Uncle Ned lowered himself and sat next to her. He reached out his hand to her opposite shoulder and pulled her to him in a sideways hug. What had been uncomfortable for her at first was welcome now. She sobbed in his embrace.

"I didn't mean to yell at you, Katy girl. I'm not disappointed with you. It's just—I'm not used to having somebody else around, especially a kid. You have so much to learn and I'm the one to teach you. You've had eleven years to learn being a kid, and I've only had months to learn to be a dad, so give me a chance, will ya?

"When I was a kid, my parents' word was law. That means that I did what I was told, even if it made no sense. So I guess I expect you to do the same. I don't tell you to do things for the fun of being in charge. I do it so you, so we, can survive out here."

Kate pulled away from him because her back began to hurt. She looked at him. "I'm ready to obey. I don't need to know why."

"Oh, Katy. You can question. I don't believe in blind obedience. That means just obeying without understanding. You will not always understand why I tell you to do something, but I will try to tell you some of the whys. I don't expect your obedience so I can feel good about being the boss. Your obedience is not just for my sake, but yours as well."

He pointed to her snowshoes. "Now put the snowshoes on again. It is necessary that you can easily put them on and take them off. That's why we practice. One day, it will be second nature to you, like brushing your teeth. You won't even have to think about it."

After several more successful tries at putting the snowshoes on and taking them off, he led her out on to the porch and showed her how to walk. She was to lift her feet and keep the fronts of the snowshoes elevated so she didn't dip them into the snow and fall forward on her face.

"Speed isn't important—careful walking is. If you fall in deep snow like we have today, you will have a difficult time getting back up. It will be very hard for me to help you."

"I'm only a little girl."

"It's survival. You fall in deep snow, especially alone, you could die out here. The wilderness is unforgiving, and the sooner you accept that fact, the better.

"I will break trail, which will make it easier for you, but you must stay in my track. Don't go to one side or the other."

It was awkward and hard walking to the truck, following in Uncle Ned's tracks. He had already dug the truck out, probably before she had gotten up. First, she did as he instructed—clean the snowshoes off each time you use them, then she dragged herself into the truck after placing her now-cleaned snowshoes behind her seat in the pickup.

"Okay, put your snowshoes back on. We're heading back to the cabin."

She glared at him.

"Don't give me that look. This is all part of your training. You need to learn how to put your snowshoes on, take them off, clean off the snow, and stow them. Once you do these steps over and over, you will be able to do them almost without thinking."

They snowshoed back to the cabin. By that time, she was exhausted. The rest of that day and the next, they practiced putting her snowshoes on and taking them off. They walked around outside the cabin in their front yard. He had her walk in deep snow where he hadn't broken trail, showing her how hard it was. He emphasized how important it was to be careful and to move slowly so that the front of her snowshoes didn't go in the snow and cause her to fall forward.

One time, Kate fell face-first into the snow. She expected an immediate hand to help her up, but it didn't come. She lifted her head and cried out, "Uncle Ned, help me."

She began to panic. Why wasn't he helping? Had something happened to him?

Her heart raced—hot tears mingled with the cold snow. She began to shiver. "Uncle Ned, help."

"I'm right here, Katy, but I want you to try to get up."

She couldn't—why wasn't he helping her?

Finally, she felt his strong hands grasp her and pull her back on her feet.

"That's why we don't hurry—not on snowshoes. You saw how hard it is to get up by yourself. We will keep practicing. One day, you will be able to get up from a fall by yourself. Don't worry, you *will* get it."

He generally shut the generator off earlier in the evening in the colder months since he could keep food cold out in the woodshed. He dried some food items and smoked others so they wouldn't need the generator all the time.

They used kerosene lanterns when the generator was not running. He kept busy most evenings. In the winter, he did inside things. One of his tasks was making "sticks"—the torches he used at night outside for light as well as to keep dangerous animals away.

Uncle Ned's "sticks" had a fancier name—he called them pine knot torches. He showed her how to make them, but she didn't think she would ever need that skill. Still, he repeatedly showed her.

He took a large, sharp knife and pounded the knife into the larger end of the stick with a short stick. Kate thought it odd he didn't use his hammer. He explained his use of the stick as something one could use out in the woods. It was a wilderness skill, he said, and if one were out in the wilderness, they probably left their hammer home.

After pounding the knife into the torch's end several inches, it was split into two halves. Uncle Ned pushed some small sticks between the halves. He then wiggled the knife out of the stick's end. He repeated the process, splitting the halves, making four nearly equal quarters. After placing more small sticks in the spaces between the quarters, he pulled his knife out.

He then placed wood shavings he had cut from a stump in the woods into the spaces, stuffing them tightly in. He did this to each of his torches.

Uncle Ned took his time. "It's always better to take your time, Katy. You never know when your life will depend on the job you did beforehand."

He didn't make her use the knife, but he did have her place the sticks and shavings into the spaces between the quarters. She doubted she'd ever master the art of making a torch, but he made sure she knew how to use one. She had to watch him light several using the woodstove.

He then made her light several torches so she could light them easily. She also practiced carrying them around outside to learn the way to safely hold them so the flaming pieces didn't fall on her hand and burn her.

She did learn that they had to use pine, one with a lot of resin on it. The stumps he used for some of the shavings had lots and lots of resin in them. The resin would ignite quickly and the torch would burn for quite some time, often longer than he would last splitting wood by hand.

He took her outside with a lit torch so she could see how it gave light. "There's not much danger from one of these in winter. However, when snow isn't covering the ground, burning resin can fall on to leaves and pine needles. You could easily start a forest fire, which might destroy the cabin and kill many animals. A wildfire could spread to other homes far away or even to town."

He put the torch out in the snow. "You can also stuff the burning end into dirt, which will put it out. Water can work, but it sometimes takes a lot—these things will burn in a rainstorm or a snowstorm, so shoving it into the dirt is a better way to put it out. But since the dirt is covered in snow now, I used snow."

Sometimes his lessons were repetitious, occasionally to the point of being annoying. She often had them long before he quit.

She tried to be respectful of his teaching, but once her face betrayed her. He looked at her, then replied to the unspoken comment. "Katy, don't make light of what I'm sayin' or get tired of it. Some 'o this is too important to chance you not getting. You need to know it so well that it's second nature."

"I don't think I'll ever need to know how to use a, um, what did you call these?"

"Exactly. You need to know this better than you do. Pine knot torches are what we call them."

During the winter months, he generally did his after-dinner work first, then spent some time reading. Sometimes he read to himself, and other times he and Kate enjoyed reading together. She tried to do most of her homework at school where she had light or when she first got home to use what daylight remained. They generally went to bed early in order to conserve generator fuel.

He usually did not make more than two or three torches in an evening, nor did he do them every day. He did, however, make quite a large stack, which he kept out in the woodshed. He would have plenty.

Another lesson he tried to teach her was knot tying. He showed her various knots and how they worked. He gave her lessons all year round, over and over. It was frustrating, but she never could remember what went where when. Even his "the rabbit goes around the hole, then in the hole, etc." never seemed to help.

She figured she really didn't need to know how to tie knots since she was a girl. She couldn't imagine why she *would* need to do it.

One evening, he was chattier than normal. He sat mending a hole in a sock. "In the old days, people would sit around the fireplace or woodstove on a winter evening, the man reading, the mother might be knitting or working on spinning yarn, and the children would be listening while they played.

"Not like today, when the kids are doing something, and the parents are off doing something else. They don't do things together like folks used to."

"Like we do, Uncle Ned?"

He smiled as he looked into her eyes. "Yeah, Katy girl, like we do. I know this place ain't what you're used to, but I love having you here."

"It is a lot different, but I like watching you and hearing you talk." She remembered her parents hadn't done much *with* her. They gave her things, but often left her alone so they could go off and do something else.

He grinned mischievously. "You like hearing me except when I keep reviewing. Well, keep listening, even when you think you know everything I'm talking about. For one thing, you may not know as much as you think. For another, I like teaching you, so keep listening."

"I will."

He kept them busy with chores, instruction, reading, and conversation. Kate didn't have time to think about what she lost, and she was so tired that she fell into a heavy sleep every night.

***

Dr. Baer sat back. "Wow. So, Kate, can you make, what did you call those things? Pine something?"

"Pine knot torches, Dr. Baer. I can't say I can make them, even though I think I know how. Uncle Ned never had me use the knife on them. He was probably afraid I'd cut myself, although I used knives to process fish and game."

"I never heard of pine knot torches. It sounds interesting, though. So, Kate, you survived the long Montana winters without succumbing to cabin fever or falling into depression."

"Yes, I did, thanks to Uncle Ned."

"That's quite a lot for a child to learn. Did you feel overwhelmed?"

She thought for a minute. "Not really. All the kids at school already knew these things, so I wanted to know them too. I just got irritated when Uncle Ned would force me to practice something repeatedly when I thought I knew how to do it. But now I know it had to be second nature."

"Yes, when something is important, we need to know how to respond the right way instinctively."

She blinked. "Are you giving me a psychology lesson?"

He pushed his glasses up and smiled. "Maybe." Then he sobered. "It's true that once we instinctively react negatively to something, we need to learn and practice the correct reaction to it."

"Hmm … Sounds hard."

"Nothing you can't handle after learning all those difficult lessons as a child."

She gave him a small smile. "I never did get knot tying, though."

FIVE

AT her next session with Dr. Baer, Kate spoke first. "I want to describe more of my experiences in my new home."

"Wouldn't it be better to get the hard things over with, then go back and pick up where we left off?" He looked at her kindly.

"Dr. Baer, for you to understand, you need to see the whole picture. Besides, I need to tell you the background to give me time to get my courage up." She rubbed her hands together.

"Works for me. Go on."

"So I was the new kid at school." She shifted in her seat and gave her pant leg a yank to straighten an annoying wrinkle.

"Did the other kids accept you?" His soft voice and kind eyes gave her courage to go on.

"It was grudging at first." Kate remembered her first year in the Pickerel school. "Those kids had known each other since they were babies, most of them. They grew up hunting, trapping, snowshoeing, all that country stuff I knew nothing about. I was the 'city kid.' "

Kate was deep into her first year in the Pickerel school. The other students talked to her, but she wasn't really included. She was an outsider, and she was bewildered at the treatment she received. Almost all of the attention that her fellow students paid her was superficial. It took her a few years to understand their concept of "outsiders."

The prevailing attitude in Pickerel was that outsiders would come for a while, then find out that they were not able to cope with the long, harsh winters, lack of city conveniences, wide-open spaces, and many dangers lurking just outside their front doors. Outsiders generally left in a year, or even a few months. Her fellow students figured she was one of those who would soon leave. They saved their relational energy for those who were there for the long haul.

It was a difficult time for her. Previously, she had been popular, part of the "in crowd." Here she was on the "outside," except for one boy who *did* give her attention.

The problem with Roger was that his attention was the negative kind. She had always been sheltered from bad kids, having had protective parents. Now she was on her own—in new and unfamiliar territory. Roger had singled her out to harass her since she was new.

He was big for his age and used his size to intimidate others. He was one grade above her, but he was on the playground when she was and walked the same way she did to Uncle Ned's truck at Harrison's store where he normally picked her up. Roger pushed her over frequently, knocked her books out of her hands, and called her names.

Her mother had fought her battles for her, but now she was on her own. She didn't know what to do.

"How was school?" Uncle Ned asked one afternoon.

"Okay, I guess," Kate said, brushing the snow off her books from Roger's latest attack. She didn't want to bother her uncle, since he had enough to do just keeping food on the table.

She suffered in silence for several weeks. Then one day, Roger pushed her really hard toward a mountain of snow. She did a face plant—her books went flying and were buried in the snow. He just laughed at her plight and left.

She got up, brushed the snow from her face, clothes, and dug her books out of the snow.

"C'mere!" a voice spoke.

Kate turned to see a young woman, seemingly in her mid-twenties, looking at her.

"Come with me," the woman commanded.

"I … I have to go," Kate said, turning away.

"You're Ned's kid." The woman said, more a statement than a question. "He's in the hardware store. We have time."

"Yeah, but I don't know you," Kate said. "My mom always said not to trust strangers."

"Up here, we got no strangers," the woman said. "We need to help each other. I know Ned got a bad deal. I never liked that woman who took his house. I knew she was bad. I don't know why everybody believed her, but I didn't. Name's Mary. I know that Roger kid. He's a brat, just like his older brother."

"He has an older brother? How old are you?"

"I'm nineteen. And yes, Roger has four other brothers. The Tatums are all a bunch of trouble." She motioned for Kate to follow her.

Kate entered Mary's shop, rather, gym. There was no one else there.

Mary showed Kate some self-defense moves and how to punch without hurting her hand or wrist. Kate was nervous about the idea of fighting. She was sure she would get the worst of it or get in trouble, probably both.

"I was bullied too. By one of Roger's older brothers, no less. I told on him. He was punished, but he still got me. So I learned self-defense like I'm showing you. The next time he came after me, I ran like I was scared. He ran after me. I stopped suddenly, whirled around and hit him as hard as I could right in his face! I broke his nose—and I'm not recommending that—but the bullying stopped."

Kate shook her head. She was no fighter. "I'm going to speak with Mrs. Pratt tomorrow."

"I hope your way works," Mary said, shaking her head. "People like Roger understand one thing—force, not punishment. If you need more ideas, come see me."

Kate kept her bullying from Uncle Ned. The following day, she visited the principal's office. Mrs. Pratt was sympathetic, and said she would look into it.

As Kate left the office, Roger sidled up to her and snarled in her ear, "Rat me out? You're gonna get it after school!" Then he was gone.

All day Kate couldn't concentrate on her classes. She was petrified. Before the final bell, she put her books and papers in her backpack, ready to race out the door. The bell sounded, and she ran for the door past a surprised Mrs. Pratt. Kate ran and ran, but she heard someone running behind her. A glance back told her it was Roger. He was gaining on her. She would not make it to the hardware store before he caught her.

As she neared a row of houses, she glanced at a pile of boards she had passed many times before. An idea sprang to her mind, and she slowed a bit to allow Roger to get closer. Just before he reached her, she whipped out a board to trip him. It worked. He fell flat on his face, and she dashed away. When she glanced back, he was on her heels again, now angrier than ever.

She remembered Mary's treatment of Roger's brother. Just before Roger could grab her, she stopped suddenly, whirled and punched him as hard as she could, hitting him right between the eyes. He stopped, stood still, then fell to his knees, blood pouring from his nose.

A group of other children gathered around, as did a few adults from the stores, including Mary. All the spectators clapped. Roger's face turned red. He got up and pushed his way through the crowd.

After that, Kate was no longer the "odd man out," as Uncle Ned called it. She was a hero. Roger left her alone after that. In fact, he left school soon thereafter. Kate guessed he could no longer live with the fact he had been bested by a girl. Whatever the reason for Roger's absence, with him gone, peace came to Pickerel's school.

The other kids gathered around Kate, not just physically, but began to include her in conversations. She had broken into their tight circle. She was still the "city girl," but they began to share with her what life there was like and how to not just survive, but to actually thrive in it. Even though her nickname most often used by the other children was "city girl," she didn't mind. It was now used with affection, so she took pride in it.

Mary took the liberty of walking with Kate to Uncle Ned's truck a few days later. "Hey, Ned!" Mary called. "Your girl here is pretty special!"

Kate blushed at the compliment.

"I know that," Uncle Ned said. "Known it all along."

"That's not what I mean," Mary said. "Kate took out a bully all by herself and now she's a hero."

"Really?"

Kate was afraid he'd be angry.

"Yep. Tell him, Kate." Mary urged.

When Kate finished, Uncle Ned gave Mary a sharp look and asked, "I wonder where she learned such things. Any ideas, Mary?"

Mary shook her head. "No idea," she said, giving a sideways wink at Kate.

"Mmmm," was all Uncle Ned said.

The truck ride was quiet for a ways. Uncle Ned broke the silence. "Katy, you ever have a problem again at school, I expect you to tell me, you hear?" His voice was sharp. "Don't *wait* to tell me, either. I can't help what I don't know."

"I didn't want to bother you. I know you have enough problems and now you have me to take care of."

"Katy, you aren't a problem." He stopped the truck right in the middle of the road. Turning to look her in the eyes, he said, "Don't you know I love you like my own? Don't you know you have given me a purpose for living?" He began driving again.

When they were getting supper, Uncle Ned was whistling. She couldn't understand why until he spoke. "My Katy," he said. "My Katy a warrior." He shook his head and went on whistling.

SIX

"SO, what are we going to talk about today?" Dr. Baer asked.

"Just going to continue with my life up until … until … bad things …" Kate said.

Her voice lowered, and he leaned forward to catch her words. "I … you need to know what my life was like so you … can cure me." She rubbed her forehead. "Talking about life leading up … helps me, a little, at least. Starting slow … the story leads to hard things."

He nodded and leaned back. "Take your time."

She took a deep breath and blew it out. "I survived my first winter. Spring was coming, the snow was lessening. My uncle did a lot of hunting and trapping to supplement his meager income and supply us with food, especially rabbits."

"Did you find it gross?" he asked. "I think I would get sick, or didn't you have to do the dirty work?"

"I learned early on to catch fish, as well as clean them. I was grossed out in the beginning, but his insistence that it was necessary for our survival and his absolute refusal to help me enabled me to clean fish."

"Did you have to clean the rabbits too?"

She smiled. "Do you even have to ask?"

***

When Uncle Ned came home from one of his hunts, he tossed a rabbit on the kitchen table. "Now for a lesson on cleaning game," he said. He drew the large knife from its sheath by his waist. He cut the animal open, pulled the insides out, and placed them in a bucket. He separated the meat from the skin and washed the meat, then placed it in a container and put it in the refrigerator. Kate felt ill, barely keeping lunch down.

He looked at her. "Get your coat on. I'll show you where we dump this bucket. Here, you carry it."

He grabbed his rifle and stepped out the door, and she followed with the smelly bucket. They walked a long way from the cabin in a direction opposite from the truck toward the woods.

"Why are we walking so far? Are we going hunting?" She pointed at his rifle.

"Spring is a great time. The snow begins to melt, the cold lessens, and plants eventually begin to come out. Something else comes out in spring."

"What?"

"Bears come out of their dens, hungry after their long winter. They have very keen noses. They can smell things humans cannot. They can smell our food, as well as what is left from our hunting." He tapped the bucket Kate carried.

"You may have noticed that I always have a gun handy. And when I'm out splitting wood, I usually have one of my pine knot torches going, always at night, but even during the day. We have to take precautions.

"I always go out prepared, especially when I'm doing something bears find interesting, like delivering a delicious meal such as this." He again tapped the bucket she held. He grinned at her. She grimaced back, trying not to barf her own guts out.

Finally, they came to a large hole in the ground several feet into the woods. He took the bucket from her and dumped its contents into the hole. He kicked at the frozen dirt pile beside the hole to break off some chunks of dirt. He stomped on them to break them into smaller pieces and pushed the dirt into the hole, covering what he'd just dumped in.

They returned to the cabin. He instructed her on how to prepare a stew, cutting up carrots, celery, onions, potatoes, and adding broth. "Now for the meat." He pulled out the rabbit and showed her how to cut the meat into chunks and add it to the stew.

She found the stew quite good and almost forgot the gross process. Of course, he had to spoil it. He looked at her and said, "The next one you can clean."

She didn't know if he were joking or serious.

"I'm not kidding around. It's part of your education up here. Most people here hunt."

"But, why? I see why you do, but the people in town don't have to hunt for food. They have jobs and—"

"Many people around here hunt, at least those who grew up here. It's part of our culture—it's what we do. It is partly for sport, but we don't waste what we take. The fur can be used to keep us warm in winter, the heads and sometimes other parts are used as home decor." With a flourish of his arm, he pointed out a deer head mounted on the wall.

The next Saturday was a beautiful spring day, warmer than it had been in a while. The snow had melted enough to make snowshoeing unnecessary.

He slung one rifle over his shoulder and took another one in his hands. She had asked before why he needed two. He explained that the one over his shoulder was for smaller game, such as rabbits. It fired a smaller bullet. For larger animals, such as a deer or to defend against a hungry bear, he would use the rifle in his hands, which fired a larger bullet. Today he was looking for rabbits, but he carried the larger rifle for defense.

Just before he stepped through the door, he turned to her. "Stay in the house. You can read, plus work on dinner. There's dishes to do, plus I think I saw some homework that needs doin'."

She nodded.

"I may be a long time. Stay in the house."

She did her homework and read until she was tired of reading. Still, he hadn't come. She did all she could for dinner before he came home. She gazed out the window. It looked beautiful, inviting. She wouldn't have to go very far. She would be near the cabin. It would be like obeying, wouldn't it? It was still cold, so she pulled on her ski pants. Then she put her boots on.

Kate stepped out the door onto the stoop, pulled the door shut, and stepped down to the ground. She walked toward the pickup. She heard the birds and tried to see the ones making the calls. She walked some more. Once, she did glance back and was astonished to see how far away the cabin was. Still, it was beautiful out, the trees and fresh air were so much better than being in the stuffy cabin. She twirled around with her hands in the air. Then out of the corner of her eye she noticed movement off in the trees.

She stopped and peered into the woods. She made out what looked like a dog, a good-sized gray one. There was more than one, maybe four. The one she had seen first looked at her, bared his teeth and … snarled. Then she realized it wasn't a dog.

Wolves! She whirled and bolted for the cabin. The wolves howled behind her.

Her throat tightened and her stomach was in knots. She ran as fast as her young legs could go in the spring snow, panicking. The cabin was getting closer, but it was still too far away. She glanced back. The lead wolf was nearly upon her. She sped up, even faster, but would it be enough? She was almost to the step of the stoop—the wolf snapped, grabbing her ski pants! She tripped on the step, tearing her pants. She felt the hot breath of the wolf. She was about to die! She burst into tears and screamed in terror.

She closed her eyes, hoping it wouldn't hurt to be eaten by a wolf. She heard shouting, then a rifle shot. Another! Another! The wolf on her was gone. She started to push herself up on her elbows when all of a sudden, she was grabbed by the back of her coat and lifted hurriedly across the narrow stoop and into the cabin. She was plopped onto the floor. The door slammed shut with her inside and Uncle Ned outside firing his rifle over and over. He then came back in.

Kate, trembling all over, sat up and looked into Uncle Ned's face. He looked absolutely furious.

His eyes blazed and his voice was sterner than ever. "I told you to stay in the cabin. You don't know enough about life up here to go wandering about by yourself. If I hadn't come back just now, you could have gotten bitten, torn up, maybe even killed. Death by wolves isn't likely much fun because they might not do it quick. When I tell you to do something, you need to do it."

Tears filled her eyes. "I'm sorry. I'm so sorry. I'll never disobey you again!"

Uncle Ned put his rifles up on their pegs on the wall, then sat down on his chair. He put his head in his hands and began sobbing, crying.

She couldn't believe her eyes nor her ears— her tough old uncle, crying.

She went softly over to him and put her hand on his arm. "I'm really, really sorry, Uncle Ned. Please forgive me."

He lifted his tear-filled eyes to hers. "You don't understand, do you, Katy? I love you so much, I guess I need you. I don't know what I'd do if something happened to you. I know you don't understand, but …"

"I understand love, Uncle Ned, and I know you love me."

He gathered her in his arms and continued to cry as she clung tightly to him. Finally he stopped crying and wiped his eyes with his handkerchief. He kissed her head and stood, then pulled one rifle down from its peg and reloaded it.

"Always ready for visitors," he said. Kate had heard the joke enough to know that "visitors" meant trouble, like hungry bears, or—she shivered—wolves.

"Jeremy at school said wolves won't hurt people," Kate said, "so why did these wolves try to eat me?"

"Jeremy is bigger than you—size makes a difference. Besides, Jeremy knows not to run from wolves."

"But you never told me not to run from wolves."

"No, but I did tell you to stay in the cabin. When I tell you something like that, you'd best obey. It could mean life or death for you, or at least injury.

"Wolves don't generally attack healthy adults, but children by themselves or someone weak and hurt are more at risk, but the real problem is that you ran. If you act like prey, the animals they eat, they will treat you like prey. Deer run from wolves and the wolves chase them, just as they did when you ran."

"So if I don't run, what do I do?"

"I'll tell you another time. I think you've learned your lesson. Let's get dinner going."

When Monday rolled around, Kate got ready for school, but she didn't put her ski pants on. Uncle Ned reached down and picked them up. "You forgot these."

She frowned. "I don't want to go with wolf-torn pants. Everybody will tease me when I have to explain how they got ripped. I'll be the 'city girl' all over again."

"Yep. Maybe that will teach you the importance of obeying." Seeing the determined set of his jaw, she knew she wasn't going to win.

Her schoolmates had a good laugh over her "wolf pants." Some of the boys began calling her "wolf bait" until Mr. Meyers, one of their teachers, stepped in. "Kate could have been killed," he said sternly. "Just because none of you have had a close encounter with wolves doesn't mean you're better than Kate. Luckier, maybe, but not better."

One evening, Uncle Ned sat Kate down. "It's time I explained some things. You now know how wolves act when you run from them. Any other dangerous animal is apt to treat you the same way if you run. There are several critters out there that you need to be mindful of. I can assure you that Jeremy or any of the others at school only go in the woods with some sort of gun in case of trouble.

"Wolves generally aren't a problem. If you meet one or several, do not run. Stand up straight, act and make yourself look bigger. Make some noise and throw objects at the wolf. Act like you are a threat to it. Stay calm, back away from the wolf, but keep looking into its eyes. Never turn your back on a wolf and for heaven's sake, don't run from it," he said.

She nodded vigorously.

"We do have cougars or mountain lions here in Montana. They are big cats that occasionally do attack people. If you ever see one, you face it and back away slowly. Never turn your back. If it approaches, make loud noises and make yourself look bigger by spreading your jacket or raising your arms. Like the wolves, do not run from it. And if it runs at you, throw rocks or sticks at it if you don't have a gun. Cougars don't like prey that fights back.

"There is one kind of venomous snake in Montana. That is the Prairie, or Western, Rattlesnake. We're kind of close to the area they are in, but we're not as likely to see them as people in other parts of the state are. But, as a precaution, I'll explain about them. You always look before you step or place your hand. Never reach into a hole in the ground or reach into bushes. If you hear a buzzing sound, back away. A rattlesnake shakes its tail which makes that buzzing sound. It means 'Stay away! Danger!'

"We have black bears and grizzly bears around here. Black bears act differently than grizzly bears. A black bear will sometimes pretend to charge, called a bluff charge, but not really attack, but if one does attack, you fight back. You never run, but stand your ground and make noise. In fact, it is a good idea to make noise in the woods so that you don't surprise a bear.

"Now a grizzly, on the other hand, is a different story. They're typically brown, but don't count on that. The easiest thing to identify them is they have a large shoulder hump. Look for the hump. If one of those attacks you, you play dead, lying on your stomach, covering your neck with your hands interlocked together and keeping your elbows close to your head. A grizzly may poke at you and may bite or claw, but if you play dead, they often lose interest and leave the area.

"But do you know the best protection?"

She shook her head.

"Staying in the cabin when you are told to. And not going out alone, but with someone who is armed. I don't always have a gun in town, but out here, I always have a gun on me or with me."

"I understand, and I'll obey you from now on." She hugged him tightly.

SEVEN

"WOW," Dr. Baer pushed his glasses up. "I guess you have reasons for nightmares, Kate."

"No, the nightmares come from other circumstances. We're getting closer, much as I hate to go there."

"You're doing great. I'm really impressed with how much you learned at such a young age."

She shrugged. "I loved Uncle Ned, so I tried to please him. Also the kids at school knew all kinds of survival skills, so I tried to keep up with them."

"Speaking of school, how were things going with your peers?"

"I lost my outsider status when I socked that bully," Kate said. "Although I was the hero for many months, I had no really close friend until a new girl came to town.

"Her name was Rosita Ramos. She was the only girl in her family and the eldest child. She suffered the same fate as I had as the new kid. I took her under my wing and we became good friends. I often asked Uncle Ned if I could go to her house after

school, and he could then pick me up later than normal."

***

Kate spent many after school afternoons at Rosita's. Kate's friendship helped smooth the way for Rosita to have a shorter stint as the "new kid."

Kate began to call Rosita's mom "Mama Juanita" or just Mama. Mrs. Ramos was warm and affectionate, treating Kate like a mother would. It felt so wonderful for Kate to have an "adopted" mom and sister.

One evening, Mama invited Kate and Uncle Ned for dinner with their family. After dinner, the girls ran upstairs. Mama was in the kitchen cleaning up, and Uncle Ned and Mr. Ramos were talking in the den. The girls were sitting on the stairs secretly listening to what the adults were talking about.

Uncle Ned spoke to Mr. Ramos, "I don't know what's come over Katy. She's irritable, cries at the drop of a hat, moody. Frankly, I'm bewildered. She didn't used to be this way. She's been a fairly happy child. I wonder if something's going on that I don't know about."

"I know, girls. Boys are so much easier. I'll have Juanita talk to her."

When the conversation changed to the weather and town politics, the girls went to Rosita's room.

Kate was upset. "I'm not irritable and moody! I can't believe he said that."

Rosita giggled. "You are right now."

Kate sighed. "I think I just miss having a family. I mean, I love Uncle Ned, but ... well, I don't know what's wrong."

"You're perfect," Rosita said and gave her a hug. "Want to play?"

A few days later, Mama took Kate aside and explained the changes her body would soon be going through and how to handle them. Kate was embarrassed, but then she was really glad to be prepared. How awful if she didn't know about this because obviously Uncle Ned didn't know either. It made her feel even closer to Mama.

Kate loved spending time at the Ramos' house, and during the summer she often stayed overnight. She seemed to fit right in with the family. Many times she helped Rosita watch her younger brothers, Enrique and Benito, and Mr. Ramos paid her. That gave her some spending money. So Uncle Ned allowed her to stay often.

One day, after babysitting, Kate walked into the cabin. "Uncle Ned, I have something for you." She pulled dollar bills out of her pocket and placed them on the table.

"What's this?"

"It's my babysitting money. I want to help out. I know you need money and—"

"Oh, Katy. We aren't rich by any means, but we're not poor either. I appreciate the thought and you are very generous, but I want you to keep your money." He rummaged around and handed her a can to hold it in. "If I ever need it, I'll ask you, all right? But for now, it's yours to keep."

When December came, Kate asked Mama to help her think of a gift for Uncle Ned for Christmas. Mama had excellent ideas and together they came up with a couple of items that would be perfect. Kate kissed Mama on the cheek. She could barely wait for Uncle Ned to open his gifts.

Kate hoped Uncle Ned would like her gifts. She didn't expect anything from him since money was so tight. Plus, last year, with all the changes in her life, there hadn't been any gifts or celebration. Maybe that was just how he celebrated Christmas, by not celebrating it.

Well, no matter what *he* did, she would celebrate. She had a nice meal planned. She would enjoy giving him her gifts even if he didn't reciprocate. It would be okay. No, it *had* to be okay. It was just the way it was.

It was funny, she mused. When she lived with her parents, it was always about what she was going to get, but now she was more concerned with someone else. She would have liked to receive a present, but what she was going to *give* was more important and exciting.

Besides, Kate knew Uncle Ned struggled just to make ends meet and although he was too proud to take her babysitting money, he had enough to do providing food and other necessities. If she wanted or needed something, she had her babysitting money.

Anyway, that was the way it was.

Finally, Christmas day arrived. After breakfast and cleanup, she told him to sit down. She handed him a present. "There is a condition for this one," she said. "You have to throw out your old ones."

He gave her a puzzled look, but opened the present. Then he laughed.

" 'Bout time to throw the old ones out." He pulled his old ratty handkerchief out of his pocket. He got up, walked to the trash can, and threw it out. Returning to his seat, he sat and pulled the brand-new handkerchiefs out of the package. He smelled one and, smiling broadly at her, put it in his pocket. "I'll throw the other ones out, I promise, Katy girl."

"Here's something else," she said, handing him another present.

"Any conditions on this one?" He threw her a sideways grin, pausing before ripping off the wrapping paper.

She laughed and shook her head, smiling widely.

When he opened the next present, he gasped. He withdrew a beautiful sling from the box.

"You have a sling for one of your rifles, but not for the other one," she said. "Now you have one for both."

He carefully examined the sling, then went to his rifle and attached it. He was humming and fussing with the sling, adjusting it to fit and trying it on, clearly enjoying himself.

"Merry Christmas, Uncle Ned." She smiled, and tried to choke down the knot in her throat. It didn't matter that she wasn't getting anything. This was *his* Christmas.

Warmth filled her heart as she watched him. He was so different than her parents. They hardly ever seemed to like her gifts to them, but would go on to the next present without much comment or enthusiasm. Her uncle, on the other hand, fussed with his sling, humming as he did.

Suddenly, his humming stopped. She looked at him, her brow furrowed. "Is something wrong?"

"Sit down," he said sternly.

Startled, Kate obeyed. His voice had sounded angry. What had she done wrong? Her eyebrows arched.

He laughed. "Don't look so serious, Katy girl. I almost forgot. I have something for you. You can open it, but I will have to show you some things before you use it. Here you go." He handed her a long package.

Kate tore into the package, throwing the wrapping paper down, then opened the plain box. She pulled out a new rifle—a .22 caliber. She gasped and looked up at him.

"Many people up here hunt to provide more food for their family. I thought you ought to start learning. Besides, you need to understand how to protect yourself out here."

She stroked the sleek barrel, hardly believing he trusted her with it.

"That's not for big game like deer or bear, but for the smaller ones, like rabbits and squirrels. When you understand how to use this, we'll move on to other, more powerful ones."

"I can't believe it." Kate admired the gun from every angle. She would be like the other kids, learning to hunt and take care of herself out here in the wilderness. More than that, however, was that he had given her a present after all. All her worry and trying to convince herself that it was okay she wasn't getting anything was swept away.

She carefully laid her new rifle down, leaped up from her seat, and threw her arms around his neck. "Thank you. Thank you. Thank you. You're so sweet."

His eyes shone and his eyes twinkled even more than they had when she gave him his presents. She realized at that moment, more than she had before, he loved her very much.

Uncle Ned, the only person willing to take her in, loved her. Loved her more tangibly, more obviously, than her parents or other relatives. Realizing that made it the best Christmas ever.

During the winter, Kate took a hunter safety course and learned gun safety rules. Her uncle's instruction was much more thorough. He showed her how to load and unload her rifle, and how to handle it safely for herself and others. He showed her how to clean and maintain it.

Finally, he allowed her to shoot. She practiced aiming at still targets to get used to her rifle, how it handled, and improve her aim. She was terrible at first, but with practice over months of diligent effort, she became a fair shot.

"Now on to moving targets," he said. The first hunt produced one rabbit for stew, but he was the one who got it. The next hunt she didn't get one either.

"The kids at school talk about how many *deer* they've shot, and I can't even get a dumb rabbit." She folded her arms and flopped on a chair.

"The kids at school have been using guns all their lives. Anything worth doing takes time, Katy. You don't have to be like someone else. Just be Katy, that's enough."

Kate smiled a little. "Okay."

"Learning to hunt rabbits is good training to hunt other animals. And rabbits aren't dumb. A lot of people hunt rabbits with a shotgun, using shot which has many pellets, instead of one bullet like your .22. I want you to learn to aim and take your time, so we're doing it the hard way. Then when we move on to larger rifles for larger animals, you will have better aim."

"You make it look easy," Kate said, scowling.

"I have been hunting for a long time. Nobody is *born* knowing how to hunt. It takes a lot of practice learned over many years. It takes time to learn how to walk quietly in the woods. You have to learn patience, to wait for an opportunity. It's like fishing—you learn what to do and wait, all while enjoying the woods with its beauty, sounds, and peacefulness."

Kate practiced for months. Finally, she shot a rabbit. She was ecstatic.

"All right, Katy." He patted her on the back.

She cleaned it and didn't think twice since by now she had processed so many. She carried the bucket of entrails out to the dumping spot with him walking along. As always, he was armed and vigilant.

"You've had deer and rabbit. If I can get a bear, you can try that as well."

"I like deer and rabbit. Maybe I'll like bear, too, but aren't they dangerous to hunt? I hear the kids in school talking about bear attacks. Someone's uncle, I think, was attacked by a bear and is still in the hospital. I don't think I'd want to hunt something that could hurt me. And I don't like the idea of you maybe getting hurt by a bear."

"If you're thinking of the same incident I am, then it was a grizzly that attacked the man. We can't hunt them legally, since they are protected by law. The only kind of bears we're allowed to hunt out here are black bears, which are not quite as dangerous as a grizzly. Although a bear is a bear, and any bear is a very powerful animal."

"But if grizzly bears are so dangerous, shouldn't we get rid of them?" Her voice quavered.

"Grizzly bears are beautiful creatures. We shouldn't go around shooting them just because they *could* bring harm to us. Part of our responsibility is understanding how to live in peace with grizzlies. The only time we would shoot one is in defense either of ourselves or someone else. You know I always have a gun with me when I step outside. Grizzlies are the main reason for that precaution, although some other animals could also be a problem.

"Another thing. Remember how I told you to stay in the cabin and you disobeyed and had the wolf encounter?"

Kate nodded, wondering why he was bringing that up again. She'd learned her lesson.

"Katy, I'm not bringing that up to scold you again. I'm only trying to make a point. As important as staying in the cabin was, so is this instruction—do not ever go hunting alone. Two hunters are much better than one. If one gets in trouble, especially with a grizzly, the other one can help out."

Kate nodded, but her inquisitive mind and independent streak would not let it go. "But you hunt by yourself."

"That's true, but there's no one to hunt with me. I am extra careful, so that will have to do."

"What about your friend at the hardware store?"

"I already told you about him. James Harrison thinks I'm an abuser of women. Even if he did want to go out with me, which I doubt, I don't want to go out with him."

"I can't imagine not having Rosita for a friend just because we had an argument."

"It's more complicated." His voice was firm, flat, like always when he didn't want to talk about something.

"If it's as dangerous as you seem to think and the kids at school say, then I wish you wouldn't go out alone." She wasn't backing down. "Just ask him, will you?"

Uncle Ned, stubborn as ever, shook his head.

If *he* wouldn't take the first step, then it was up to her. She would talk with Mr. Harrison herself. She lay in bed plotting a plan of action. She would ask to go to Rosita's, but go to the hardware store first. It wasn't really a lie.

At school, Kate told Rosita she would be over, but she had to do an errand first. Rosita offered to accompany her, but Kate insisted she go alone. If Mr. Harrison were half as stubborn or reluctant to talk about difficult subjects as Uncle Ned, it would be hard enough to get him to talk to her alone.

When Kate walked into the hardware store, Mr. Harrison greeted her. "Your uncle isn't here, Kate."

"I know, Mr. Harrison. Actually I wanted to see you."

"Oh?"

"I don't like Uncle Ned going off hunting by himself."

"The stubborn old coot. I've told him I'll go with him. He holds a big grudge about—"

"I know the story. He told me. Why didn't you believe him, instead of that woman? He said you'd been friends for years."

He rubbed the stubble on his chin. He blew out a long breath. "I've tried to mend the fences, Kate, but Ned won't budge. I really hurt him, I know, but he won't accept my apologies."

"I would hate to think that a fight with my friend could destroy our friendship."

"Well, Kate, it was more than a fight. I chose to believe a relative stranger over a guy I've known for many years. I … I really don't know why."

"Did you ever apologize, really apologize?" She gazed steadily into his eyes.

"I tried, but Ned won't accept it. The betrayal festers like a wound that won't heal. I see the bitterness written all over his face."

"Well, sometimes people *say* they're sorry, but they don't really mean—"

"Katy," Uncle Ned said sharply, startling her. "What are you doing here? I thought you were going to Rosita's."

Kate was caught—another lie would get her in deeper.

"Ned," Mr. Harrison said, "Kate was trying to get me to apologize to you."

"What'd you do *this* time, James Harrison?" He scowled.

"Ned, I … I don't have anything to say, except that I'm sorry. It's all I can offer you. It's been eating at me and I know it has at you, although you won't ever admit it." He flung his arms up. "I'm talking about the *incident*."

"Why are you getting involved in this, Katy? It doesn't concern you." Uncle Ned's voice was harsh, and he looked at her crossly. "Up here in Montana, people mind their own business."

Despite her fear, Kate replied, "I did it for you, Uncle Ned. I hate when you go out hunting alone, especially when the bears are out. I just thought … if you and Mr. Harrison were friends again, then you wouldn't have to go out alone. I'm sorry I lied, but I knew if I asked, you would say no and I worry every time you go out alone."

Then, her voice breaking, Kate said softly, "I was orphaned once. I don't want to be again. Please, Uncle Ned."

The hard face Uncle Ned wore in the presence of the townspeople, and especially around James Harrison, cracked a little. "Katy, I see your point. But I can't just forget it happened. Harrison here was one of the most vocal against me. How can I forget his betrayal after Brenda betrayed me?"

"Ned," Mr. Harrison said, "you don't have to forget. I've kicked myself a million times. I'd just like a chance to be your friend again. Letting my terrible offense go doesn't mean you forget. It just means we can be friends, like we were."

"It will never be the same." His voice was flat.

Looking into his eyes, Kate thought she detected a softening, and—was it possible? Did his eyes glisten a little?

"Uncle Ned, Mary told me forgiveness doesn't mean it never happened and relationships change because of hurts, but holding on to bitterness hurts us more than anyone else."

"The girl makes valid points, James," Uncle Ned said, as his glistening eyes filled.

"You never called me 'James,' Ned, since the—"

"Yeah," Uncle Ned said, then broke down sobbing. Kate threw her arms around him. She motioned for Mr. Harrison to join in.

Kate felt Uncle Ned's arm raise, and she pulled back enough to see him touch his friend's back. Mr. Harrison began to cry. He sobbed onto Uncle Ned's shoulder. "I'm so sorry. I'm so sorry."

"I know, James," Uncle Ned replied. "Me, too."

Rosita showed up at the hardware store, and looked shocked at the two grown men crying their eyes out.

Kate swiftly went to her friend. "Sorry, Rosita, I had to tell Mr. Harrison something. We'll have to get together tomorrow, maybe?"

"You told me you were coming over today. I thought you were my friend," Rosita said, pouting as usual when things didn't go her way.

"I am your friend, Rosita. I was trying to patch up two old friends," Kate replied, pointing her thumb at the men. "Emphasis on the *old*."

Rosita smiled and she began giggling right along with Kate.

"Hey, who're you calling old?" Uncle Ned asked.

"Yeah," Mr. Harrison said.

"You two have lots to talk about. I'll be at Rosita's." Kate and Rosita shot out the door.

Later on the ride home, Uncle Ned spoke. "I forgive you for your deception, Katy, and it had a great outcome, but I don't appreciate being lied to. I don't know how you could have done it differently, but I still don't like deception. I need to be able to trust you."

"I know. I'm sorry, but I'm not, you know what I mean?"

"Teenagers," he replied. By now, Kate generally could accurately interpret his voice, so she knew he was not angry.

"I'm not a teenager yet."

"Technically, but you're acting like one, and as you might know, I calls 'em like I sees 'em. Teenagers." He shook his head.

Despite her act of deception having such a great outcome, she knew it had to be an exception. She had to honor the trust he placed in her. She doubted her parents would have trusted her as much as he did.

He gave her a lot of freedom and allowed her to question him. He did have his lines, however—like deception, respecting the dangers in the wilderness, and obeying. She understood obedience was a protection for them both, especially her.

***

Dr. Baer leaned back in his chair. "Wow, you sure got away with stuff."

"Hey. I didn't get away with anything."

"What punishment did Uncle Ned give you? It sounded like you got away with your deception."

"I didn't get punished, but disappointing him was enough to make me never want to do it again. I wouldn't hurt that old man for the world. And Uncle Ned never brought it up again."

"Did Mr. Harrison go hunting with him after that?"

"Yes. I was so relieved. I couldn't bear to lose him. He meant the world to me." She suddenly remembered the letter, and pain stabbed her heart.

Dr. Baer rubbed his chin, then shook his head slightly. "You seem to still care about him. I don't understand why you wouldn't read his letter."

She exhaled loudly. "I told you it's a long story. I can't just jump to the end. It wouldn't make sense and … I'm not ready yet."

"That's fine. You know what you feel comfortable sharing or not. I appreciate all you've told me
so far." He smiled warmly.

She nodded. "Next time, we'll get a bit farther. I promise."

EIGHT

KATE hadn't hung out with Mary for quite a while. She spent most of her free time helping Rosita with schoolwork, as well as babysitting the boys. Also she was learning how to survive in the wilderness, keeping up with her studies, and was exhausted every night.

Kate felt ashamed that she had let so much time go by without seeing Mary. Probably by now Mary wouldn't want anything to do with her. Still, she made up her mind to try. She told Uncle Ned she'd like to see Mary and told Rosita she wouldn't see her that day. Rosita pouted, but Kate refused to be manipulated.

"Come on, Rosita," Kate said, as they walked toward Rosita's home. "I see you nearly every day. I haven't seen Mary for months."

Rosita only tossed her head, continued to ignore Kate, and walked on when Kate stopped in front of Mary's place.

Kate stepped into Mary's shop and looked around.

"Well, hi there, Kate," Mary said.

"I ... I ..." Kate broke down in tears.

Mary rushed to her and pulled her chin up. "Whatever is the matter, Kate?"

"You … you helped me with that bully, Mary, and I've … I haven't been by to see you. I'm so sorry. It's been months since I've been by. That's no way to treat a friend, I know …"

Mary placed her fingers on Kate's lips. "Shhhh," she said softly. "Enough already."

"But I haven't been by. You must think I'm terrible." Tears ran down her face.

"Stop already, will you? I know you have a friend. I see you two nearly every school day. It's natural to want to be with someone your own age."

"Yeah, but you saved my life."

"My, aren't you the dramatic one. Look, Kate, how about we forget how long it's been and just pick up where we left off?"

"I'd like that," Kate said and sniffled.

"Good. So, go back outside and come back in, and we'll start over."

Kate obeyed. When she entered, Mary said, "Kate, nice to see you. How've you been?"

"Quite well, thank you, Mary."

They both giggled and Kate breathed a sigh of relief.

"You have any bully trouble lately?"

Kate shook her head. "Roger left school soon after I punched him. His gang fell apart, so we're good."

Mary nodded. "That's good, but I want to teach you more self-defense. Roger isn't the only one to cause trouble around here. This is rough country. Knowing how to defend yourself is a necessity. They may call us the fairer sex, but if they come looking for trouble, we need to show them we can kick their butts."

"I would like that, but I don't have much money."

"For you, it's free." Mary grinned.

"Then I'll work super hard to learn."

Mary began teaching Kate how to break holds, even by a stronger attacker, and how to fight back if someone really meant harm. She made Kate practice.

Mary offered to teach Rosita for free too. But Rosita declined, declaring that fighting was unladylike. Kate, on the other hand, ate it up, all while hoping she would never need it, and wishing she were more ladylike. She was a tomboy and there was no changing that. Most boys in Pickerel were respectful toward the girls, but not all of them. If someone threatened her, she needed to be ready.

Mary told Kate she'd heard rumors of revenge to repay Kate for humiliating Roger, even though it had happened long ago. Roger's older brother, Richard, had a score to settle with Mary as well. The Tatums held onto grudges, and sometimes even took revenge years later. Hopefully nothing would happen, but Mary wanted to be sure Kate was well-prepared.

Months of regular training and conditioning were making Kate into an athletic young woman capable of holding her own in a fight. They prepared for a battle which she and her trainer both hoped she would never be in.

One day, Kate suggested that she and Rosita take a walk. The weather was warm for a Montana spring. Snow lay on the ground in places, but bare spots were beginning to show through. Instead of walking down the street as they normally would, Kate decided to duck down an alley and come out in the partially open area behind the shops. She had never explored back here. She knew it was safe since wild animals didn't come into town.

As Kate and Rosita walked, they came to a small wooded area. It was a gorgeous spot and Kate marvelled at the beauty, and at the fact that she had been in Pickerel for so long and had never discovered this serene place.

Rosita hesitated to enter the woods.

Kate tugged on her arm. "C'mon, Rosita—no bears in here. They like the wilderness out where I live. They wouldn't come so close to town."

Rosita's dark eyes flashed. "It's not just bears, Kate. Sometimes, you're too reckless, taking chances."

"What do you mean?"

"Oh, I don't know. How about walking along the top of the stone wall on the way home from school?"

"That's nothing."

"It's a lot if you fell—you'd break your neck. You sass the boys at school. If you tick one of them off enough, they'll beat you up."

"Nah, Rosita, they know better."

Rosita had little idea of the self-defense skills Kate now possessed. Just let some boy try it, she mused, quite pleased with herself. She felt powerful, in control. Yeah, just let some boy try it.

Suddenly, Kate was grabbed from behind. She whirled and swung, but her masked assailant ducked and her swing missed, throwing her off balance. Her attacker aimed a punch at her nose, but she pulled away a little before he smashed it. Blood spurted—it was probably fractured. Whoever this was, he meant business. She kicked him hard in the shin.

"Ow." He yelped in a familiar voice.

Kate recognized her former bully—Roger. She kicked him in the other shin. As he bent over, Kate pulled the mask off his head.

Just then, Kate heard Rosita cry out. Kate turned and saw someone punching her friend. Roger landed another punch, this time hitting Kate's jaw hard. Blood on her face, she faced Roger. It didn't look as though she'd done much damage.

"You leave my friend out of this," Kate screamed in fury.

Rosita screamed, but it was different—it was a scream of terror and pain.

Kate instantly went on the offensive and struck hard so she could go to Rosita's aid. Roger swung. Kate ducked, throwing him off balance. She kicked him hard between the legs. He groaned and fell to his knees. She aimed a careful kick at his face. He fell to the ground and lay still.

Kate shot toward Rosita. Whoever was attacking her was kicking her as she lay on the ground. For whatever reason, the attackers had put the bigger one on the person less able to defend herself. Kate attacked the person kicking Rosita.

Soon, others joined the fight against her. Kate was getting the worst of it, since she was outnumbered. At least, they were leaving Rosita out of it— for now anyway.

Kate held her own against three attackers. The moves Mary had taught her came in handy because her attackers couldn't get through her defenses very well. They deflected many of her strikes, but she did manage to hit one of them hard enough that he retreated out of the fight. That left two to deal with, but time was on their side. She was shaking from the terror and shock. Her strength was ebbing quickly.

The larger of the two attackers drew his arm back for a devastating blow. Since he was a grown man, his strike would put her down. She scrambled to avoid it. Just before his powerful fist connected, he groaned and dropped to the ground. Kate was relieved to see Mary on top of him, pummeling him with her fists.

With him out of the picture, Kate turned to the remaining assailant and kicked him in the shin. She followed up with another to the opposite shin. He bellowed and hobbled away. The first one was headed back into the fight and he had company. This group was too large for Kate plus Mary. They would soon be overwhelmed. Kate was learning about Tatum revenge the hard way. Her stubbornness, her refusal to take Roger's abuse, and her arrogance about her fighting prowess put her and Rosita in grave danger. Especially Rosita. And now Mary.

But whatever the outcome, she would resist to the best of her ability. The enemy was going to win, but not without a fight. She was a warrior—Uncle Ned had said so.

Kate saw Mary stop pummeling the assailant she had knocked over and attack the ones coming to join the fight.

Just before the others reached Kate, a rifle cracked!

"If anyone touches any of the girls, the next bullet will be *in* him." Uncle Ned stood, holding his rifle ready. "Katy, get up and check Rosita. Don't any of you others move. I know who you are and what this is about. Mary, pull off their masks."

"Gladly."

"Tatums," Uncle Ned said with contempt. His rifle was steadily pointed in their direction. "All of you but one is over eighteen. Attacking minors will get you in adult trouble. Richard Tatum, you're going away for this."

"You got no proof." Richard denied everything. "An' no witnesses. I never hit nobody."

"I saw you." Kate said.

"So did I." Mary pointed at him. "I saw you kick that poor girl on the ground. That's two witnesses. You're history."

While Mary was arguing with Richard, Kate rushed over to see how badly Rosita was hurt. Her friend was curled up in a fetal position, crying and groaning. Kate looked to Uncle Ned for help.

Too late she saw that Roger had gotten up and snuck behind everyone. He had a massive rock in his hand and was about to smash it on Uncle Ned's head. She opened her mouth to scream. Crack! Another rifle went off. Roger crumpled to the ground. The rock hit Uncle Ned's shoulder and grazed his back and leg.

Everyone turned to see James Harrison twenty or so yards away, rifle in hand.

A Montana state trooper bolted forward. "All right, everybody. No one move. Men, put your weapons down!"

"He shot my brother." Richard Tatum pointed at Harrison.

The trooper nodded. "In order to prevent a life-threatening assault, deadly force becomes necessary. If he had struck this man's head with that rock, it's likely he would have killed him. He will be charged with assault with attempt to commit murder."

Richard kept shaking his head, pleading with the officer. "Murder, no, Roger wouldn't do that. Please spare him—he's my little brother."

In the distance, Kate heard a helicopter. Holding Rosita's hand, she watched it land in the clearing outside the woods. Two orderlies rushed out, and made Kate step away. They checked Rosita, carefully lifted her on a stretcher, and loaded her in the helicopter. In moments she was whisked away into the sky.

Kate gripped Uncle Ned's hand. "Is Rosita going to be okay?"

He shook his head. "I don't know, but she's in good hands." He rubbed his shoulder with a grimace.

The police arrested all the attackers, except for Roger—they placed a sheet over him. Richard, his face contorted and tear-streaked, sobbed as he was led away in handcuffs.

"I've got to tell Mama," Kate said suddenly.

Mary shook her head. "No need—the Ramos' knew about a possible attack."

Kate's mouth dropped open as she looked at Mary.

Mary shrugged. "I called the state police before I came out here. I told them we probably would need a helicopter because I expected serious injuries. I warned the Ramos' that Rosita might be in danger. I asked them to round up help."

"How did you know about this?" a trooper asked.

"I'd heard a rumor about the Tatums vowing revenge and I saw a couple of them in town. When I saw Kate and Rosita go out here, I feared the worst. I knew this was just the place for an ambush," Mary replied. "I knew it could have been a false alarm, but I didn't think it was."

The police told Mr. Harrison that he acted in defense of another person and no charges would be filed. Then they escorted the Ramos' away.

Uncle Ned rubbed his shoulder. "James, I owe you one."

Mr. Harrison shook his head. "Nah. Just a partial payment on a debt."

Uncle Ned grinned at his old friend. "That debt was settled, remember?"

The grin faded when his eyes fell on Kate. "Katy, we gotta get you patched up."

She nodded, wiping blood from her face. Her nose hurt so badly, she hoped it wasn't broken. She could hardly move her left forearm. It was probably fractured. Pain shot throughout her body where she had been kicked or punched.

Before they left, Uncle Ned nodded to Mary. "Thanks for taking action. Your quick thinking saved Kate and Rosita."

"I know. We wouldn't want any repeats, would we, Ned?"

He shook his head. "No."

Kate wondered at the conversation. It seemed Mary and Uncle Ned shared a secret of some kind.

The drive to the doctor's clinic jolted every painful part of her body.

She was rushed in for X-rays, then had to sit and wait for the results. She was utterly exhausted and leaned against Uncle Ned. He held her silently.

Eventually the doctor had to put her left arm in a cast. Her nose and a couple of her ribs were fractured but they would have to heal on their own.

The doctor was firm. "No roughhousing. No hunting nor using the arm until I clear you."

Kate's heart sank. That meant they would be eating Uncle Ned's cooking. She had become a better cook than he and they both enjoyed her talent. She would also miss out on hunting. She needed all the practice she could get to be ready for deer season.

Kate couldn't sleep that night from pain and worry. What if the Ramos' wouldn't let her friendship with Rosita continue? What if Rosita blamed *her*? If only she hadn't punched Roger, if only she hadn't gone the back way, then Rosita would not have been hurt. If only. If only. Rosita had warned her about her recklessness, and now Rosita was badly hurt. Kate didn't know how badly, but Rosita didn't deserve to be hurt at all. Kate's body and heart ached all night.

After breakfast, Uncle Ned took her to see Rosita.

Enrique answered the door. "They're in her room." He pointed, and Kate walked softly toward Rosita's room.

Uncle Ned squeezed Kate's arm and stopped walking. "You go ahead, Katy."

Kate looked in, but Rosita was not there. Her parents were holding each other on the bed. She hesitatingly approached them, tears in her eyes. When she found her voice, it came out in a timid whisper. "Mama, I'm so sorry. It's my fault."

Mr. and Mrs. Ramos both reached out and grasped her good hand.

"We don't blame you," Mama said. "Rosita told us how brave you were, coming to her defense against a grown man. Rosita is going to be okay. She's got some broken bones, including ribs, and one of them punctured her lung. So they need to watch her at the hospital."

"When we get Rosita home, we want you to come over," Mr. Ramos said.

Mama stroked her good arm. "How are you, Kate?"

"I have a broken arm and fractured ribs. And a fractured nose. My body is bruised all over, but at least I'm walking."

Mama gave her a kiss and said to go home and rest.

A few days later, the police stopped by the cabin to let Uncle Ned and Kate know that all the attackers had been arrested and charged with assault. Kate was safe now.

When Kate returned to school ten days later, kids swarmed her everywhere she went. Tales of her exploits in the face of overwhelming odds grew and grew, seemingly greater with each telling, becoming more than the actual events, it seemed.

She took it mostly in stride, knowing she had done a brave thing, but after a while, she just wanted it to die down. Thankfully, it finally did. The other students, even the boys, recognized she was a force to be reckoned with and any fight with her was likely to end badly for them.

Rosita had not come home yet, so after school, Kate went to see Mary. She had asked Uncle Ned first if she could—no more deceptions. She desperately wanted to ask Mary about the secret she and Uncle Ned alluded to, but thought it was likely none of her business.

Still, Kate's curiosity would not let go. She greeted Mary and they began their session of training and conditioning.

"All right, Kate. Spit it out."

"What?"

"Oh, come on, you're so transparent. You're dying to say or ask something. What is it?"

Kate placed her hands on her hips. "I know it's not my business, but you and Uncle Ned keep talking about some secret, and I can't help wondering what it is."

Mary sighed, looking deeply into Kate's eyes. "Well, then, time for a story. Better sit down. Everyone knows anyway. I just don't care to go over it again. But perhaps my story will reinforce the importance of our training."

Mary looked over Kate's head, as if she peered into the past. "After I punched Richard Tatum those several years ago, I feared something might happen along the lines of what happened to you and Rosita, but the fight never materialized. Then Richard began acting like he wanted to be friends, then more, like be my boyfriend. I'd never really had a serious one and I cautiously began to trust him. He acted sorry that he'd bullied me."

Kate saw the anger in Mary's eyes. "We walked in the woods where you were attacked. One afternoon, he tried to kiss me. I pushed him away. I said I wasn't ready for that. He got angry and stormed away. He wouldn't talk to me at school. I cried a lot. One day, a friend passed me a note that warned me I was in danger. Apparently, she had heard Richard talking, bragging about what he planned to do to me. I couldn't believe it—he had acted like he wanted to be my boyfriend, and now he was contemplating harming me?"

Kate's eyes were riveted on Mary. "What did he do?"

"One afternoon, I took a walk out in the woods. I suppose any thinking person would believe I had forgotten the threat hanging over me, but the woods are my peaceful place. I felt relaxed out there and due to the stress, I needed to relax.

"I walked past one of the largest trees. Suddenly, I was grabbed from behind and thrown to the ground. I tried to look to see who it was, but I was slapped across the face—hard, so hard I almost blacked out. He grabbed my jeans and yanked them. I screamed and screamed as his intent became clear. I looked at his face, but he had a mask on and I couldn't tell for sure, but I thought it was Richard Tatum."

The horror her friend had faced unnerved Kate. "Did he …?"

"Yes, Kate, he raped me. When he was done, he punched me in my face and left me there, unconscious. When I came to, I painfully walked back into town and a friend drove me to the hospital. The state police came and took my statement, but nothing ever came of it since Richard had a legitimate alibi. Anyway, I determined that I would never be vulnerable again. That's when I learned self-defense and opened my gym."

Mary's face softened. "I'm sorry to speak of such things to you. You're just a kid, so innocent."

Kate shook her head vigorously. "I am *not* a kid. I need to know what life is about."

Mary nodded, then gently touched Kate's face. "But you are so … innocent. I hesitated to tell you."

"I've heard things like this before, so I'm not as innocent as you imagine. But, anyway, thanks for answering my rude question."

Mary gestured with her arm, making a sweeping motion. "Kate, most people around here, and most anyplace, I imagine, are good and will help you. There are only a few bad people, but they do exist, here and everywhere. That's why I work out in my gym and why I'm helping you be ready to defend yourself. It's important that you know whether the fight is a half-hearted one or is life-and-death. If it is as serious as I just shared, you do whatever you can to survive. Understand?"

Kate nodded, but shuddered at the mere possibility of such an attack. She was more determined than ever to be ready for anything as she continued to train with Mary.

Mary's training was both physical and mental. One had to have not only fighting skills, but perhaps even more important was preparation of one's mind. One had to be willing to harm someone in order to defend themselves or another person.

She reminded Kate that the police were good and helpful, but given the amount of territory they had to cover, help might arrive too late in an attack. That made self-reliance in a dangerous situation imperative. The intended victim had to be able to hold off, or even defeat, an attack in case help was late in coming. It was no criticism of the police, merely a fact of life in spread-out Montana. Even in another setting, however, such skills were good to have.

"We live in rough country, Kate, but I would not wish to live anywhere else. The air is clear, not too much traffic or people. Most folks will help you. Those who hurt others are few and far between, but we must prepare to meet them with strength if and when they show up."

NINE

DR. BAER leaned forward. "That was a terrible attack on you and Rosita. I'm sure it had a significant impact on you. I'd like to hear more about it. Did you and Rosita remain friends afterwards? Also, is that why you have nightmares?"

Kate rubbed her forehead. "First, no, that's not the source of my current nightmares. I'm slowly making my way to that part of the story. But yes, I did have nightmares after that. I worked extra hard on self-defense moves so I wouldn't feel so helpless. I also didn't feel cocky anymore. After what Mary said, I knew there were men who would see young girls as easy prey. And with all the open spaces, they could get away with attacking them. So I viewed everyone differently after that. I guess I became an adult at that point."

"What about Rosita?"

"She finally healed enough to come home. We both were extremely sore for a long time while our bones healed, and we didn't have the easy friendship we once had. She was really traumatized for a while and wouldn't go anywhere without an adult. Eventually, it got so I could coax her out for a walk occasionally, just the two of us. But we both were hypersensitive to everything and everyone around us. We never walked anywhere without a lot of people around. We didn't hang out nearly every school day like we used to or talk much even at school."

"I'm sorry, Kate. That's a hard lesson to learn as a young teen. But I'm grateful you and Rosita were not hurt more than you were. I'm sure the trauma took a while to overcome."

She nodded. "More for Rosita than me. But she still didn't want to take self-defense classes. We kind of drifted apart because I was spending so much of my free time working out or hunting. She didn't hunt either. At least she had a caring family who looked out for her. Her brothers started learning how to fight after that."

He nodded. "What happened next?"

"Well, let's see. Nothing significant ... I was adjusting, learning more, and working hard at everything. I'll jump to when I was fifteen."

***

Kate was gaining ground in learning to hunt larger game, especially deer. She learned the right way to hit the deer to kill it quickly so that the animal would not suffer, nor run too far. She learned how to use a shotgun for multiple uses. Uncle Ned called it the best all-around weapon for hunting and defense. One could use shot for small game such as birds or rabbits, and slugs for larger game, such as deer and bear.

Uncle Ned drilled into her head which shells did what. He especially pointed out the slugs that would stop a bear—most likely, he added. Kate didn't like the "most likely" part, but Uncle Ned stressed that precaution was the best defense against grizzlies, but in a pinch, well-placed slugs were most likely to stop an attack.

Kate now was the proud owner of her own rifles, a .22 for small game, and a .30-30 for deer and bear. That Christmas, Uncle Ned presented her with her own 12 gauge shotgun. She had learned on his, and now he felt she was ready for her own. She also gained the skill necessary to safely handle and clean her uncle's handguns, but she was not given her own.

Kate knew how to thoroughly clean her firearms. She understood how to store them safely, how to carry them so neither she nor others were endangered, and how to load and unload them. She had become a fairly good shot, maybe not as good as the locals who had grown up there, but good enough to bag small game regularly, and she also had had successful deer hunts.

She was severely forbidden to go out hunting by herself. She wanted to be given that privilege, but Uncle Ned stubbornly refused.

"Grown men go out in pairs," Uncle Ned said, for the millionth time.

"You don't," Kate replied, hands on her hips.

He fixed her with a steely gaze. "I take James Harrison when he's available. We need meat more often than he can come. Besides, I know what I'm doing."

Kate quoted her uncle's words right back at him. " 'Bears are tricky—no matter how much we think we know about them, they can outwit us.' " Kate's growing confidence in her own abilities added to her normal rebelliousness.

He frowned sternly at her. She felt a twinge. He didn't look at her like that very often.

"Do you remember the wolves, Katy? You don't know everything about life up here. The locals, as you call them, have learned about life here since they were babies and toddlers."

She felt anger flood her veins and held her hand up. "I thought you promised to never bring that up again."

He shouted back at her. "I thought you respected me enough to take my word for it. You think you're so smart and tough. Well, let me tell you, girl, there's more here than you know. This country is rough and too tough to take on when you don't understand it. Even when you *do*, sometimes the wilderness or bears win."

His voice softened, and his face began to relax. "I'm sorry for yelling at you, but I don't like being yelled at either, and I don't like being disrespected and disobeyed.

"A few years before you came here, two out-of-town greenhorns went grizzly hunting. They did know something about hunting, but the finer points were lost on them. They should have spent the money for a guide, but they said they knew what they were doing. They ignored the suggestions some of the locals offered, one of which was to hunt black bears instead of grizzlies. Grizzly hunting is illegal, not to mention dangerous."

"What happened?"

"They did shoot a grizzly, sure enough, but they didn't kill it. That bear likely rushed at them, covering the yards separating them in seconds. I wasn't there, nor was anyone else, but we know how grizzlies generally respond. If that's what happened, one or both men would have been knocked to the ground, then mauled, bitten, clawed. Anyway, a very angry wounded grizzly came upon another man walking with his dog."

Kate gasped.

"Well, this man was a local, and he was armed. He shot the bear, killing it before it could harm him or his dog. A wounded grizzly is twice as dangerous. When he's hurt, he's really angry at who or what he thinks hurt him and he will attack anyone."

"What about the greenhorns?"

"By the time they were found, they were both quite dead. Whether they were killed during the attack or died from blood loss, I don't know. My point is that I need you to not get arrogant about what you know or what you *think* you know. You must always, always, always be careful. I am always careful—I make sure my guns are cleaned and working well. I carry extra bullets and shells. I am always alert to my surroundings. I pay attention to the other animals, the small ones who go quiet when someone or something large is on the prowl.

"I am proud as anything at how you are becoming an accomplished woodswoman. Your proficiency in hunting is quite good. You can sneak up on prey much better now. There is much to be happy about in your progress. It's just when you think you know all there is to know that you can become careless—not just you, but anyone."

He looked into her eyes. "We—you and I—are not in competition. I'm glad to teach you all I know, and even for you to surpass me. I mean that. But you must never think you've arrived, because that's when you're headed for disaster. I've seen it happen. Woods-wise people think they know it all, get careless, and meet with disaster. Disaster often means dead."

She sat down at the table, caressing her rifle while he continued.

"I remember one fellow, very experienced, who boasted of what he knew to anyone who would listen. Someone found him by the side of a river, far from where his pack was. Maybe he had attempted to cross, but underestimated the force of the river, or just fell in, or some other cause. Whether it was his own fault or some freak occurrence, he drowned in a river not particularly dangerous, nor unfamiliar to him. I have no way to prove his arrogance got him killed, but I'm sure it didn't help."

He placed his rough hands on her shoulder. "You're good, Katy, but no one is exempt from continual vigilance, from always being aware of one's surroundings. You must always keep in your mind that despite your best effort, intentions, and skill, something quite unexpected could arise. You never totally arrive.

"Out here, we are always learning, always watching. Comparing yourself with me or with anyone misses the point. We all need to strive to be the best we can be."

Competent as she was, she knew he was right. If something unexpected happened and she was alone, it could easily mean death. Remember the wolves, her conscience reminded her. Remember the Tatums. No matter how experienced she was, there were many situations she truly couldn't handle alone.

She blew out a breath and looked up. "Okay, Uncle Ned. I won't go out alone, and I won't think I know it all."

He squeezed her shoulder. "That's my girl. I love you too much to lose you."

She reached up and squeezed his hand. "I love you too."

Kate was becoming an accomplished expert in wilderness living. She could fish and hunt, clean what she caught, and prepare it for eating. She could clean her guns as well as Uncle Ned and knew what ammunition went for which gun and what gun and bullet were needed for what kind of game.

"Well, Katy," Uncle Ned said one day, "we have one more thing you need to learn in order to live out here."

She did a quick checklist in her head. What did Uncle Ned do that she didn't? She couldn't think of a thing.

Uncle Ned laughed. "C'mon! I'll show you."

They walked down to the truck and climbed in. Uncle Ned turned the truck around and backed it up toward the cabin toward the edge of the parking lot. He then shut it off. "Here, Katy, trade places."

Her mouth dropped open. "Seriously? You're going to teach me to drive?"

"Sure enough."

Soon Kate was sitting behind the wheel of his beloved truck. Her heart began to beat faster. Her hands shook. Although she did not possess her license or even a permit, apparently she was going to learn to drive.

He showed her how to start the truck, how to run the windshield wipers, and how to turn on the lights, both inside and out. She had often adjusted the heater, so she needed very little review of that. She regularly looked over at the speedometer when Uncle

Ned was driving, and had been finding out the odometer reading for his records, so those were familiar.

He pointed at a gauge. "This here is the tachometer. When you rev the engine—"

"Wait, what?"

"Push the accelerator."

She just looked at him.

"The pedal on the right is the accelerator. It makes the car go. Push it."

She did just what he said and the engine roared.

He grabbed her leg and pulled it off the pedal. "Whoa, whoa, whoa. Easy does it, girl. That's what it means to rev the engine. Not good for it, but did you see the needle on the tachometer? It registers a higher number when you rev it. Do it too much and it can really hurt the engine, so you want to be aware of not making the needle go very high."

He reviewed all the controls again in his methodical, maddening way. He was very thorough, but she had enough. This was no time to allow her rebellious streak to erupt, however, and she choked down her compelling desire to scream, *I got it—stop*. Despite her attempt, she scowled and made an odd noise in her throat.

He either didn't notice, or didn't care, for he plodded onward. He explained the pedals. "The one on the right is the accelerator. It makes the truck go. The one in the middle is the brake. That slows us down and will stop us. This here is the emergency brake. We use this when we leave the truck running, but it might roll, so we pull this on, like this. Then when we are ready to go, we release it, like so."

Kate's eyes were beginning to glaze over. She was a good learner, but too much new stuff all at once was sometimes overwhelming. It didn't help matters that he repeated stuff she already knew. It was tough to focus.

"And the pedal on the far left is the clutch. This kind of vehicle is called a—"

"Truck, I know *that*, Uncle Ned." Did he think she was dumb?

"That isn't what I was going to say, Katy. I know it's a lot of info, but you need to know all this. What I was *going* to say, is this is what we call a stick or stick shift."

He held up his finger as if he were a professor or something. She restrained herself from rolling her eyes. Her head was hurting.

He seemed to not notice, explaining that some vehicles are called automatics. His truck was not one of those, but rather was called a stick. To operate those, you had to use the far left pedal, the clutch. He said he liked sticks so he could roll it down a hill to start it if the battery went dead.

She sighed with relief when he said, "Well, enough for today."

The following day, Uncle Ned, in his thorough and maddening way, reviewed the operations of the accessories and the pedals. He showed Kate where the gears were and had her move the gearshift through all the gears.

Uncle Ned shooed her over to the passenger seat and climbed into the driver's spot. He started the truck and they were off.

She was disappointed she wasn't going to drive, but she knew he'd insist she be patient. She would have to listen to his repeated explanations, over and over, long after she had gotten it. It was torture, but complaining would get her nowhere but in trouble.

He pulled off the main road on to the road that led up to Rainbow Lake. To call it a road was generous, as it was grassy with slightly worn tire tracks. Few ventured on it since it was off the beaten path and close to Uncle Ned's land. They generally had it to themselves.

Right in the middle of the road, he stopped the truck and turned it off. He looked all around, then got out of his side and walked over to the passenger side. Kate slid over to the driver's seat. She took note of how carefully Uncle Ned surveyed his surroundings before he got out of the truck. She had often seen him do this. She knew—grizzlies were out and about. He'd seen one some months ago, but Kate had never seen one. It was one of those things you wanted to see, but then again, maybe you didn't—certainly not up close and personal.

Uncle Ned explained how you put the truck in gear, give it some gas, and ease out the clutch while increasing pressure on the accelerator. She wiped sweaty palms on her pants. This was it.

"Just try it."

Kate tried. She popped the clutch and stalled the truck.

He pointed at the ignition. "Start it again."

She did and stalled it again. After several failed attempts, he took over, although, she noticed, he checked all around outside before he stepped out. He turned the truck around and pulled out on to the main road, but instead of heading home, he drove on past their parking spot.

"Where are we going?" she asked.

"We need to charge the battery, which we do by driving. I don't want a battery that won't start the truck."

Uncle Ned spent a lot of Kate's free time over the next few weeks helping her learn to operate the truck. Finally, she was able to engage the gears without stalling. Then she practiced changing gears while moving. He refused to allow her to drive on the main road without her permit in order to prevent any problems later getting her license. Despite her protests and arguments, he was firm.

One day, while she was driving them down the path, he instructed her to drive into a wet area. She hesitated, but did as he said. As she had anticipated, the truck got stuck. He reached behind her, pulled his rifle off his rack, and stepped out of the truck, chambering a round as he did so. He motioned her to step out as well.

Uncle Ned gave her verbal instructions on what to do as he kept a watchful eye all around them. That day, she learned how to use his come-along. He gave her step-by-step instructions. First, she fastened a thick rope around a tree, then fastened the other end of the rope to the come-along. She hitched the other end of the come-along to the frame underneath the truck.

Kate cranked the handle of the come-along and was shocked that it pulled the truck out of the mud. She disassembled the come-along from the rope and the rope from the tree, and soon they were safely in the truck headed home. It was humbling to think how much she still had to learn.

After a small snowstorm, Uncle Ned took Kate driving in the snow along the path. He made her go into a skid and showed her how to correct it. She learned how to apply the brakes firmly but gently to reduce the possibility of skidding on slick surfaces and losing control of the truck. She learned how to use sand, which was kept in the pickup in a box behind the seat, to give the tires traction in slippery conditions. She discovered that ashes, of which they had a lot, also worked in place of sand. He showed her how to use boards or logs or rocks to give the tires traction when they were mired in mud or on a slippery surface.

Kate could now operate the truck, using the clutch, shifter, going from a dead stop, and working through the gears. She could get free from mud, snow, or ice.

She was becoming proficient driving in all kinds of conditions, but was still practicing on the path. Although she begged to drive on the road, Uncle Ned adamantly refused.

"If we got caught driving on the road now, it could make it harder to get your license. Listen to me. It's not just about getting caught, it's about doing what's right. You can't drive on the road until you're legal."

He caught her look as he made eye contact. "I know, Katy girl, but you'll soon be of age. Don't be in a hurry to grow up. When you get to be my age, you'll wish the birthdays quit coming so fast. Besides, doing right pays off, even if it's only having a clear conscience or not having to look over your shoulder worrying about being caught. In fact, my mom used to say, 'Doing right is its own reward, even if you get nothing else out of it'."

He suddenly stopped speaking. Kate saw the tears in his eyes and remembered him telling her how he grieved his mother's death.

Hard as it was, Kate had to be patient. The day after her sixteenth birthday, she applied for and soon received her learner's permit. Every time they went somewhere, she asked to drive. He let her, and it was not long before she had her required hours. She was on her way to becoming a fully licensed driver.

TEN

ONE day as Uncle Ned and Kate were shopping, James Harrison said, "Look, Ned, you gotta get one of these."

"What is it, Mr. Harrison?" Kate asked.

"It's a ham radio. People use them in remote areas, like where you guys live. There's no monthly phone bill, plus no risk of wires getting torn down in storms." Mr. Harrison held it up. "Besides, what're you gonna do when one of you gets hurt and you need help?"

"Katy can drive and so can I," Uncle Ned replied.

"Yeah, but with one of these, you can call for help and get someone to meet you on the drive in. What if both of you are unable to move? What if—"

Uncle Ned held up his hand. "Okay, okay, James. Enough already. I've been okay all these years without one of these gadgets, so why do I need one now?"

"Just 'cause God's been merciful to you, Ned, doesn't mean you won't need one later. You don't have to buy it from me, just get one. It'll come in handy, you'll see."

"Now, James, don't get all worked up about it. Okay, okay, so what do I gotta do to get one of these?"

"You have to have a license which you take a test for. It's not easy, but I'm sure you and even Kate could pass the exam."

She scowled at him. "I think I'll do okay on any old exam."

Mr. Harrison's eyebrows went up.

"I'm near the top of my class."

Uncle Ned laughed. "Bitten off more than you could chew, James Harrison! Katy's no slouch when it comes to smarts—got both me and you beat, that's for sure."

Although pleased at her uncle's praise, she felt her face burn. She smiled shyly at Mr. Harrison.

Both Kate and Uncle Ned studied for the test and both passed, and each received a license. Uncle Ned's call sign was to be used at their base station and his handheld radio. She had her own small radio with her own call sign.

She was surprised that Uncle Ned would join the modern world, but he assured her he agreed it was a good idea. A twenty-mile drive in a life-threatening emergency was serious. Alerting help who could meet them partway or all the way if necessary was a good idea.

Uncle Ned took an interest in learning how to use their new tool. He contacted the county emergency dispatch for practice and made Kate do it. He had her write down the procedure on a 3 x 5 card and taped it next to the radio. In the few evenings when there was nothing to do, one or the other would talk to people farther away within the state or in other states. Once or twice, they even spoke to someone in another country.

Kate wondered how he had paid for the radio, including the installation of a rather tall antenna. He hadn't even complained about the expense.

Another time at Harrison's store, Kate caught Uncle Ned looking at a propane-fueled hot water heater. When he caught her looking at him, he asked, "So, Katy, is it about time to get running water?"

That same day, he purchased a water heater and arranged for a plumber to install it, along with two propane tanks for fuel. The plumber would also furnish and connect an electric pump to the existing well and install a large pressure tank to give them running water in the cabin.

Kate couldn't believe it—running water after all these years. Still, they were dependent on the generator to run the pump to get the water inside, but the sizeable pressure tank was enough to provide for most of their needs when the generator was off. Then there was the hand pump in the kitchen still available for use in case the generator had not kept up with their usage.

Kate smiled at him. "Uncle Ned, I really appreciate all these things you're doing for my comfort, but I hope you aren't going into debt on my account."

He shook his head. "*Our* comfort. I'm enjoying being able to call for help if we ever need it. Running water is a luxury I have missed, honestly. Hot water right in the tap—wow! Much better."

Uncle Ned's eyes twinkled. "But, you're welcome. A girl shouldn't have to live without these things."

"I considered myself fortunate that I didn't have to go to the outhouse in minus 30 degrees. I've seen a couple of those when we were out hunting. Do people out here really use those horrid things?"

Uncle Ned smiled. "I did up until a few years before you came. I did get tired of going out to it, like you say, when it was 30 below. Yes, people live farther out than we do, and yes, those outhouses you saw are likely in use, even in this day and age."

"Well, I'm thankful for what we have. But I was wondering how you paid for all this. I mean, you lost your money with the house being taken away."

"Don't you worry none, Katy girl. I have some money, a couple small investments and some savings. I do get a bit here and there and sell my deerskins. I've been saving up for such things. I manage to do some odd jobs for folks—sometimes for being neighborly, sometimes I get money."

That winter, an early snowstorm blanketed the area with an abnormal amount of snow. They were snowed in, but it was not a problem, other than missing her classes. In return for a couple small tasks, Mr. Harrison allowed Rosita to use his ham radio to give Kate her assignments and to continue receiving Kate's help with her studies. The help was very short, however, so others could use the airwaves.

Uncle Ned and Kate started to break a trail out to the truck, but another snowstorm struck, and they were forced to return to the cabin. As they did, Kate's side hurt. It was odd. She could walk and keep up with her uncle normally. Today, it was an effort. Must be tired, she thought, and said nothing.

"Not unlike a few other tough winters," Uncle Ned said as they looked out the window. They had sufficient food for many days and plenty of easily accessible firewood since he had made the door directly into the woodshed.

Kate looked at the storm, then turned to Uncle Ned. "I … I don't feel so good."

"Probably hungry. I'll get dinner. You sit down."

"I'm not *that* hungry," she said, then giggled. "Ooooh. It hurts to laugh, but it *was* funny."

"Yeah, real funny," Uncle Ned replied, feigning grumpiness. "If you aren't feeling well, best get to bed. I'll get my own supper."

She made a quick stop in the bathroom and climbed the ladder to her room. Each step was agony. She concealed the pain from Uncle Ned, but she was worried. She had felt discomfort the previous day, but assumed she had overdone wood stacking or something. The pain had not lessened, but increased today. Even walking brought discomfort. Probably caught the flu, she mused. Still, something kept knocking at the door of her mind, like this was unlike any previous flu she'd had. *I need rest*, she told herself. Despite her worry, she fell into a deep sleep.

In the middle of the night, she woke up. The fire in the woodstove must be going extra hard, she thought. She was roasting. She swung her feet off her bed to stand. She saw the floor rushing at her as she collapsed. She was burning up.

Uncle Ned was at her bedside moments later. He picked her up and placed her back in bed.

"What's wrong?" he asked gently.

"My stomach hurts terribly," she said, her voice low, and teeth clenched. "I must have a fever— I feel so hot. I feel like I'm going to throw up."

"Pardon me," Uncle Ned said, and pressed on her abdomen. She yelped in pain.

"I'm not a doctor, but I think you have appendicitis. We need help."

Kate knew he'd have to start the generator in order to use the radio. She was glad he'd recently purchased a remote start for it so he didn't have to risk going out in the storm. She hoped the generator was protected enough from the snowstorm in its shed. Now she knew why Mr. Harrison insisted that they have a ham radio—and was grateful they had bought one. In a few minutes, she heard Uncle Ned call the county emergency dispatcher and tell him her symptoms.

"It's been a busy night, but we'll get an ambulance to you in about two to three hours," the dispatcher said. "We're not prepared to hike through the blizzard and snowdrifts. You've got to get her at least to the road."

Uncle Ned promised he would get her there.

He called up to her. "Katy, I'm getting the sled. I'll be right back."

"I'm not going out in my PJs," she replied. She was determined to get dressed, but the effort to just get her pajamas off was excruciating. Thankfully, she wore underwear to bed, so that was done. She managed to get a sweatshirt on, but the pants were impossible because of the pain.

The fact that her jeans were thrown in a heap on the floor, plus the fact that she liked them snug, didn't help matters. Now she was in a quandary. She needed help getting her jeans, and maybe even getting them on, but the only person available was her uncle. That would be extremely awkward.

When she heard the door open and close, she called down to him. "Uncle Ned, I need help with my pants."

"Just wear your pajamas," he said.

"No, I want to get dressed."

"Fine." She heard grumbling but couldn't make it out. While he was coming, she tried to reach her jeans on the floor, but yelped when she tried to bend. Mary's endurance training helped her remain conscious and focused despite the pain coming in sharp waves. She lay back on her bed. She did manage to get her pajama bottoms to her knees.

When he got to her bedside, she pointed toward her jeans on the floor.

"How do I do this?" he asked, reaching down to pick them up.

"Same as you," Kate replied, teeth still clenched against the pain. "But first, get my pajamas off."

His face was red, extremely so, and his hesitation revealed his concern for modesty. But he managed to remove her pajama bottoms and pull her jeans up to her thighs. Kate thought that whoever worried about a single man caring for a maturing young woman needn't have bothered.

"Uncle Ned, pull them up more," Kate said. "I can't get them over my butt since I'm lying down. I can't sit up or do anything. It hurts too much."

Uncle Ned stopped. They had to get going, she knew. He had to know, too. In emergencies, you had to forget modesty, but he was frozen into inaction. What was she to do?

He finally moved, turning his back to her and crouching down. "Put your arms around my neck. I'll stand up, pulling you to a standing position, then you can finish the jeans."

She latched onto his neck.

He managed to get her to her feet but remained turned away. She moaned and yelped, but was able to pull her jeans up the rest of the way, then zip and button them.

"It's safe now," she said, panting through the pain. "Thank you."

He turned again to her, his face terribly red.

She placed her hand on his arm. "I know it was hard for you, but it was very important to me to get dressed. And I appreciate the privacy you give me."

Now a new hurdle faced her. "I'll never get down the ladder—reaching, bending, it all hurts."

Uncle Ned quickly, yet gently, picked her up and carried her in his arms. When they reached the ladder, he set her back on her feet. "There is no time to lose."

He held her to prevent her falling to the floor. Otherwise, she would have, her strength nearly gone.

"I … I can't climb down. I'm sorry," she said, shaking. "What are we going to do?"

"*You* aren't going to climb down—I am," he replied, turning his back to her. "Arms around my neck again. You will have to hang on tight. No, not *that* tight. I have to breathe, you know."

Despite her pain, she was amazed at her uncle's ability to climb down the ladder with her clinging to his back. He did it carefully and gently, but was quick about it. She understood the necessity for hurry—she was in a really bad way. She shuddered to think what could have happened if they had not gotten the radio or the generator's remote start.

Uncle Ned took two pine knot torches and placed them into the woodstove. He then helped Kate get warm outer layers on. He lay her in the sled. He then covered her with a mammoth bear coat she had admired but never worn.

He grabbed the now-flaming torches and closed the woodstove. He opened the door of the cabin. Despite her fever, she shivered as the biting, howling wind and swirling snow blew in. How would he ever find the truck? And would he wait for help or dig the truck out and drive to the hospital?

He placed the two flaming torches into a snowbank several feet from the cabin. He then took a long rope and tied it to the post holding one side of the roof over the doorway. "Gotta find my way back," he said by way of explanation. He fastened his snowshoes to his boots. He pulled the sled with Kate in it on to the stoop and shut the cabin door.

He carried his shovel in one hand. With the other, he grabbed one of the torches—he looped the sled rope around his forearm. His pistol was in its holster at his side. Bears would be hibernating and any other dangerous critters would likely be holed up somewhere. Still, they had to take precautions. If the torch didn't deter a predator, the gun would have to do.

"Hang on, Katy. We're off."

They plunged into the teeth of the storm. Uncle Ned did not hesitate, despite the danger. Light from the torch would have normally pierced the darkness of night, but the blowing, swirling snow cut visibility to a few feet at most. Sometimes she couldn't even see him pulling the sled. Would they get lost in the storm? Could he find the truck? She gulped freezing air between spasms of pain.

Finally, they made it. He removed enough snow from the truck so he could open the passenger door. He then untied the ropes holding her on the sled and lifted her inside. "Hang on, my girl. I'll clear the tailpipe, then I can start the truck to keep you warm."

A few seconds later, he started it. She was shivering uncontrollably and the pain was unbearable from all the jostling.

"I've got to shovel to get the truck out." He closed the door.

The next thing she heard was a siren and she saw flashing lights. The back doors were open and bundled-up figures were lifting her.

Uncle Ned kissed Kate's head as she was slid into the ambulance. He told her he would follow shortly.

***

Dr. Baer was leaning forward, riveted to her story.

Kate didn't want to relive all the details of the surgery or her hospital stay. "Well, it wasn't fun having my appendix out, and they told me if we had waited much longer I might not have made it."

"How scary. I would have been out of my mind wondering if I'd ever get to the hospital."

"Uncle Ned told me later he was terrified he would lose me. I had no idea how serious it was. The pain was so intense that all I could do was force myself to keep breathing and not pass out. But I knew Uncle Ned would do whatever it took to save me. Even if we didn't have the radio, he would have driven me to the hospital in that old beat-up truck of his."

"From what you've told me about him, I'm sure he would have dragged you on the sled if he couldn't get the truck out. He would have given his life to save you."

119

She sighed. "Yes, he would have. That's one reason I feel so terrible about neglecting him." She put her hand up. "Before I talk about … any of the hard stuff, I need to give you the whole picture. Plus get up my nerve."

"That's fine." Dr. Baer sat back and rubbed his forehead. "Take your time. It really does help to know what you've been through in your life. Everyone's story is different, but yours is especially unusual."

She squirmed, picking up her purse. Before leaving, she wanted to lighten things up. She grinned. "Well, I'll tell you one thing. Mr. Harrison never let Uncle Ned forget that *he* was the one to insist we get the radio. He was so proud of himself. And he was really glad neither of us lost our lives."

ELEVEN

"HEY, Kate." It was Larry, one of her classmates. "Has your uncle told you the story of Three Toes yet?"

"Yeah, Kate," another boy said.

Caitlyn tossed her head. "You guys. That story isn't even true. Don't believe a word of it, Kate. It's just a legend—a silly, scary story told around campfires at night."

Larry glared at her, scowling. "It is so true, Caitlyn Morgan. My father said Ned Perkins told him the story as out-and-out fact. You ask him, Kate, he'll tell you. Then we'll see who's right. It won't be you, Caitlyn."

That night at supper, Kate said, "Uncle Ned, the kids at school were talking about some legend."

"Oh?"

"Yeah, Three Toes is what Larry said."

His eyes blazed. "Larry Kingsley should mind his own business."

Kate cleaned up after dinner and did her homework. Uncle Ned still hadn't said a word about her question. So she went to bed.

The next day, Larry asked Kate if she had asked her uncle.

"He said you should mind your own business, Larry," she said. "I agree with him."

"Ned's afraid, that's why he won't talk about it. You have a right to know, Kate. He's afraid. Just ask him again."

She couldn't believe what Larry said about her uncle. He was fearless. Hadn't he taken action against that pack of wolves that almost ate her? He went hunting by himself. He was prepared for anything. He couldn't be afraid, or could he?

Uncle Ned was quiet during supper, listening to her chatter on and on about school, her friends, and how happy she was living here. Finally, she stopped. "Uncle Ned, have you heard a word I've said?"

"Huh?"

She pointed a finger. "You haven't heard a word I've said, have you?"

Her uncle looked up, and she was silenced by the look in his eyes. Was it fear, or sadness, or what?

He spoke barely above a whisper. "Three Toes is no legend. It is as true as Larry says it is, maybe truer. If only I could take it back, I know I would."

She leaned forward and held her breath.

"A few years before you came to me, I was out hunting. I was going to bag me a grizzly. It's quite a feat to take one by oneself. I knew it was illegal, but I wanted to prove to myself I could do it. You know, all that macho stuff men do."

He scratched his jaw. "You're probably wondering if I thought about what my mom would say if she were around, about doing right and all that. At the time, I either forgot or pushed it out of my mind. Besides, it would be a lot of meat, a nice fur coat either for wearing or selling, and bragging rights."

He exhaled slowly, then took a deep breath. "After hunting for days without seeing anything suitable, I came upon a nice big fellow who ran before I could get a clear shot. I was angry at the thought of losing him, so I fired off a shot without taking careful aim.

"When following in the direction he'd run, I saw blood on the ground. I knew then I had wounded him. Examining the ground more carefully, I saw that his tracks were different—one of his footprints had blood and showed only three of his toes."

"Three Toes!"

"Yes. From then on, I would occasionally see that peculiar footprint and know he had been around."

Kate shuddered at the thought of a large grizzly prowling around. "Is he dangerous? And what does this have to do with a legend?"

"Three Toes is the main reason I have told you not to leave the cabin alone, not to hunt alone, and why I have taught you to keep your 12 gauge loaded at all times.

"I should have told you without being goaded into it by Larry Kingsley. It's just that I didn't want to frighten you. I thought I could keep you safe if you obeyed my rule of staying in the cabin."

"But what is the legend?"

His voice lowered into a whisper. "The legend, which is no legend, but no one believes me, is that Three Toes has sworn or vowed, or whatever it is that grizzlies do, revenge on me for shooting his toes off."

Kate laughed. Up until now, everything her uncle said had more or less made sense, not that she always agreed, but at least it had made sense. But a grizzly bear vowing revenge? It was too much.

"It is no laughing matter, as ridiculous as it sounds. I am not a crazy old coot. I'm not losing my mind. This is serious—a huge danger."

His eyes were scared and his voice was unsteady. "I have followed his tracks right past the farm where delicious cattle were there for the picking, past luscious berries, on to follow *my* footsteps all the way to this cabin. His tracks told me that he looked around, surveyed the scene and left. Although he took a deer I had hanging up, I fully believe that he was looking for only one thing—me. And I refuse to change that belief."

He lowered his gaze to the floor. When he raised his head, tears filled his eyes. "That beast knows where I live. Fortunately, I have not seen his tracks for several years. About the time you came to me, I stopped seeing them."

Her heart beat faster than usual, but she put on a brave face. "He's probably dead and his pelt graces someone's living room."

He shook his head. "I think the best we can hope for is that he left the area. I don't think there's a hunter around who could've taken him."

He described in detail what Three Toes's deformed footprint looked like.

"Katy, I cannot overemphasize the importance of not going far from the cabin and never, never, never without your 12 gauge or your rifle, especially in non-winter seasons."

"Would my 12 gauge or rifle stop Three Toes?"

"I hope so. He's a very scary specimen, *very* scary. I honestly don't know what would stop him, but I hope that several well-placed shots would do the trick. He's big, mean, and quick, plus he has a grudge. Your best bet is to stay close to the cabin and in it mostly. Watch and listen to the little animals as I taught you. If they are quiet, there's a reason. The reason may be you out hunting for them, but it may be a larger predator hunting for *you*."

Uncle Ned dropped the subject about the Three Toes legend. Kate doubted a four-footed creature was capable of what her uncle said. No wonder the townsfolk thought him a bit "off." She had to part ways with him on this one, not openly, of course, but she was pure skeptic.

Uncle Ned continued to avoid the subject of Three Toes, but constantly reminded Kate to stay in the cabin every time she was there alone. He seemed distant and preoccupied. Was he worried about a mythical beast who would leap out and maul them out of revenge? When she tried to bring up the subject to see if that was what was bothering him, he shook his head and wouldn't look at her. She feared he was slipping into some sort of mental decline.

Kate brought up her confusion about Uncle Ned with Mary. Mary was the kind of person she could talk with about anything. She would give you a straight answer, sound advice, and wouldn't think less of you for asking. Rosita was a good friend, but she was nervous and flighty. She would worry and refuse to go walking with Kate if she heard the story about a vengeful grizzly.

Mary thought for a bit, silent as she mused. "Well, everyone here in town thinks Ned's an old coot, strange in his ways," she said. "A lot of them worry about you, about how safe you are."

"He would never harm me," Kate said. "I know he loves me as he would if I were his own."

"I know that, Kate, but folks don't. They think he overreacted to the Brenda mess. They think it threw him off."

Kate flung her hands up. "It *did* throw him off."

"I know, but what I mean is they think he's crazy because of it. Refusing to live in town—even with a young one to care for, is sufficient evidence to suspect he's missing some gray matter. Then you add the Three Toes thing and they're convinced he's gone over the edge."

Kate stared at her. "Do you think it's true?"

Mary shook her head. "No, I don't buy the Three Toes revenge thing, but I know Ned Perkins. There's not much that scares him, but this legend has him spooked. He's terrified something might happen to you, which is why he tells you over and over to stay in the cabin when he's gone. Which, I might add, is a problem for your adventurous spirit."

"Don't forget rebellious." She grinned.

"That too, Kate, and I'm not making a joke. You'd best be obeying him. He knows this country better than most, even the guides. If Ned Perkins told me to stay inside, you'd better believe I'd be doing it. If he'd be concerned about a bear, even if I didn't believe all he said, I'd still follow his advice."

"You hold Uncle Ned in high regard, obviously."

"Ned Perkins is a true friend. He'll do whatever he can for someone. He's always been supportive of me.

"After I was attacked, when I was jumpy, always looking over my shoulder, too ashamed to go out, too scared to stay home, Ned took me to his cabin."

Mary smiled mischievously. "Oh, my, did the tongues wag then. They figured he was going to use me as well, I guess. People are funny. They will think the worst of someone just because of what it looks like. Ned was a perfect gentleman. He was kind and gentle and shielded me from the things I feared. One rule he insisted upon was that I remain in the cabin when he was gone. I never pushed that rule, not even for wolf-watching."

Mary smiled, tried to hold the laughter in, but it spilled out and she began giggling so much that she almost couldn't breathe.

Kate could not help but smile at the sight of her friend laughing so hard, but she was also disgruntled that others still found her disobedience so amusing.

"Anyway, Ned helped my fear settle down. He brought me back to my home and always looked in on me when he was in town. People still talked, but he and I both knew he was no more than an older brother looking out for his little sister. People finally came to that same conclusion, or kept their thoughts to themselves, and life settled back to normal."

"So you think Uncle Ned has his quirks, but he's fine. Right? Nothing I need to worry about?"

Mary smiled. "No. Your uncle is as solid and trustworthy as they come. If he wants to believe that bear has a grudge against him, it doesn't bother me. Animals are very intelligent, and bears have a sense of smell thousands of times better than humans."

"Seriously?"

"For sure. That's a fact. They even have excellent eyesight and memory. I don't believe they think like us and hold grudges, but they *are* carnivores. So you don't want to mess with bears, especially grizzlies."

Kate felt better after talking with Mary. She wasn't worried about Uncle Ned anymore. She would take his warnings about bears more seriously. She needed to research more about how good a bear's senses were.

TWELVE

LIFE continued on as Kate grew, both in age and Montana experience. The legend became a thing of the past. School was going well, and life was in a comfortable routine.

However, she was concerned about her friend Mary. She seemed distracted when Kate tried to talk with her. She wasn't like the Mary she had grown to know and love.

One day, Kate jumped right in with, "Mary, I'm worried about you. You aren't your normal upbeat self lately. What's going on?"

Mary smiled faintly. "I'm not sure, Kate. I'm just thinking about life, I guess. I mean, there's gotta be something more, right?"

"Oh, you mean like get a man?" She rolled her eyes. "Come on. Like you really need a man. Don't you have enough in your life as it is?"

"My, aren't we snippy today? Is it *that* time of the month?"

Kate scowled. "Well, I wanna know what's wrong with you."

"I said I didn't know. So now you're the judge, jury, and executioner? No, a man isn't what I need. I think I know that."

Kate smirked. "Maybe you're looking for God."

"You might just be right." Mary was dead serious.

Kate shook her head. "I was just kidding, Mary. You can't seriously be thinking that's what you're missing."

"Don't you ever wonder about God? Maybe he really does want something to do with us."

"Maybe he doesn't even exist. Yeah, that's where I am." Kate crossed her arms. "If there was a God, why did he let my parents die? No, there can't be a God."

Mary lifted an eyebrow. "Or maybe you should be asking, if there is a God, why did he bring you to nice old Uncle Ned instead of some relative who would ignore you or worse—abuse you? Or send you to an orphanage since no one wanted you?"

Kate looked away, feeling very uncomfortable. She didn't want to consider that.

"I don't know the answers to your questions, Kate, but I do know you ended up in circumstances lots better than many. So is it luck, or did someone's hand move things to make it happen? I think it takes more to not believe than to believe that God exists and does things for us."

Kate felt a storm inside of her. "Or *to* us. *That* I might be able to believe." She was surprised that she still had so much bitterness because of her life circumstances. "So my friend Mary—tough, confident, sure-of-herself Mary—has got religion."

"I didn't *get* anything, Kate," Mary replied. "You asked me what's going on, and I told you I was thinking about life. Then you go off on this tirade about God or religion or whatever. At least I'm willing to consider that there's more to life than just what we can see and touch. That makes more sense to me."

"Whatever. Sorry I brought it up. Well, I've got to go."

Soon after, a preacher came to Pickerel. Mary began attending the church which met in the town hall. Although Mary invited Kate on several occasions, she always refused.

Mary's new interest bugged Kate. Mary still tutored her in self-defense techniques and strength conditioning, but she wasn't as singularly focused on it. Religion had captivated Mary, and she constantly talked about God throughout Kate's training. It was irritating, but Kate didn't want to lose her friendship with Mary by telling her to stop talking. Instead, Kate took out her frustrations in her workouts.

One day, while Uncle Ned was out hunting, Kate was alone in the cabin. There was a knock on the door. That was strange—few people would walk the distance from the road to their cabin. Once or twice a salesman had managed it, yet left empty-handed.

Kate grabbed her uncle's 9 mm Glock with a round in the chamber, took the safety off, and held it in her right hand. Then she cautiously opened the door with her left. It was a man and a woman.

"Hi, I'm Jesse Smith and this is my wife, Jenna," the man said as he smiled at her. "Are you Kate? I'm the preacher in ..."

Kate held her hand up. "My uncle doesn't like me talking with strangers."

The woman stepped up. She had a sweet, innocent face. "We're just trying to get to know our neighbors. That's all. We can leave if you want."

Kate sighed. Might as well get it over with. She wondered if Mary had asked them to visit.

"Yes, I'm Kate. Just a minute," she said, shutting the door in their faces. She put the safety back on the 9 mm and replaced it in its holster hanging on the back of the door. She then held the door open and motioned for the smiling couple to enter.

She decided to act like the experienced local she was. Besides, it was best to take the offensive to keep them off guard so they would leave and take their religion with them. "Not too smart being out here with no weapon. I guess bein' a preacher 'n all, you just trust God and don't worry about things like bears and such."

"Oh, y'all needn't worry 'bout us," Jenna replied, patting her husband's chest. It was then Kate noticed the bulge beneath his coat—sure enough, the preacher was packing—something large, too. Three Toes better watch out, Kate mused, and had to choke down a laugh that would have taken too much effort to explain.

"Yes," Jesse said, smiling, looking at his wife. "We just came from down south. Georgia, to be more precise. We have wild pigs there and used to hunt them. It's always wise to carry a large caliber handgun just in case of emergency when hunting the pigs, so I just continued to carry when we moved up here. Legally, of course."

"Think that peashooter will stop a mad grizzly?" Kate asked, irritation overriding her normal manners.

"Well, miss, we didn't come to argue over firearms," Jesse said soothingly.

"No, you came to shove religion down my throat, mine and my uncle's. God didn't save my parents, so why should I give a hoot about him? Tell me that, preacher."

It was Jenna who replied, quietly, steadily gazing into Kate's angry face. "You are not the only person who has suffered loss."

Her soft, genuine response startled Kate. She was used to anger being met with anger. But this woman, this couple, did not retaliate. Retaliation she could understand, but not kindness. Still, her guard was up. "Maybe. But I know what I suffered—you don't. You think you understand and you were about to tell me you do, but you don't. Not one bit."

The woman persisted. "No, I *don't* think I understand exactly how you feel."

Kate didn't speak. Anger battled curiosity inside of her. She didn't know whether to snap back or ask what she meant.

Jenna spoke again, in a gentle whisper, so that Kate had to strain to catch the words. "Some years ago, I was on a train travelling alone to see my parents who were missionaries. A man asked for help and my naive self did not discern his intention to cause harm until we were between the cars. He began dragging me into the next car. I fought back, but he was too strong for me. He stumbled over something, and I seized the opportunity and kicked at him until he fell beneath the wheels. I can still hear his scream. My parents were giving their lives to *save* people, and here I had taken a life."

Jenna's eyes filled with tears. "Other passengers helped me back into the train car I had been in. I was told that people travelling alone in this area were often abducted and operated on to get organs which would be sold. The unfortunate victims often suffered injuries or even died.

"And then, I lost my parents in a senseless killing by bandits. There was no need to kill them. They were always generous to people in need. So I may not know exactly how you feel, Kate, but I have an idea of the pain of losing one's parents." Jenna's eyes were sad, yet Kate saw something else. Compassion. One wounded soul reaching out to another.

Kate smiled, being polite and all, but in her heart, she pushed Jenna's attempt away. Even if God were real, he deserved her bitterness for what he did to her parents. She deserved to hold it against him.

Jesse gently touched his wife's arm. "We have all suffered, Kate. We say this not to minimize your pain, but to help you see you are not alone."

Kate was too stunned at Jenna's story at first to give a snappy comeback, but her bitterness quickly took over. They were probably being extra nice because they wanted money.

"I, er, *we*, don't have money to give, and even if I did, I wouldn't give you any." Kate felt a twinge, knowing her uncle would scold her for being so rude.

Jesse shook his head. "We're not asking for money. We just wanted to meet you. But since you brought up your pain, we want you to know you're not alone." His voice was gentle. "God wants to be with you in your pain. He cares about you, even though you don't want him. God has given us peace, and if you're interested, we would love to share with you how you can have peace too." He stood and held his hand out to his wife.

As they made their way to the cabin door, Jenna turned and looked deeply into Kate's eyes. "Life is better with God than without him, Kate. Not easier, but better."

When Uncle Ned returned, Kate told him about the visit. He nodded, then raised an eyebrow. "Did you offer them coffee or tea or anything?"

She shook her head.

"Whether we agree with someone or not," Uncle Ned said, "we can be polite. I know you got no place for religion, but it's no excuse to be mean to those who do. And as for your friend Mary, if this religion gives her some peace, then good for her. Don't begrudge her none."

Kate wanted to argue, but she knew he was right. She just hated that religion had come to Pickerel. It changed her friend Mary and then came looking for her. But she was locked up tight.

***

"So," Dr. Baer asked, "did you ever get religion? I don't know about religion per se, but a relationship with God comes highly recommended by some."

Kate glared at him. "No. Mary got something. She kept saying it's not religion, it's God. Aren't they one and the same?"

"To some they appear to be, but no, they aren't," he replied. "There's a difference. Religion is a set of rules you follow in an attempt to get to God, whereas having a relationship with God directly is the real deal. Sounds like that's what your friend 'got.' "

She folded her arms. "You sound like an expert. Are you gonna ram it down my throat like Mary did?"

"I should think you know me better by now, Kate. Have I rammed anything down your throat?"

Kate reluctantly shook her head. Still, she was disappointed. She thought she had left God back in Pickerel, along with the other horrible memories. It was like he followed her, or at least, the idea of a God followed her. But how could an idea do that?

Dr. Baer broke into her thoughts. "I'm very interested in hearing the rest of your story." He held his hands out in front of him. "While God is very important to me, I don't force him upon my clients." He smiled warmly at her. "I do hope you will continue with this."

She bit her lip, considering her options. She had felt safe opening up to him all this time, and it was therapeutic sharing her past with someone she now trusted. If she never came back, it would have been a waste of time. He wanted to hear her story, and there was more she could share. Even though turmoil stirred inside of her, she was too far into her story to quit. She nodded. "Yes, I will." But deep down, she feared she would never find peace even with the telling of it.

***

Kate continued to visit Mary, but it wasn't comfortable like it used to be. Mary still helped Kate develop her self-defense moves, conditioning, and strengthening. But Mary constantly spoke of her peace and hope. It was "God this," and "God that."

One day during their training, Kate snapped. "Come on, Mary. I liked you better before you got religion. Now you're nearly as bad as a preacher."

Mary stopped abruptly, staring at Kate. "You're my best friend, Kate, and I'd like you to be happy, like I am. Maybe more than I am. I just know that Jesus changed my life and I'd like you to share that."

"Well, maybe I don't want it." She stood with her arms folded.

"I see," Mary said softly. "Fair enough." And that was that. Mary stopped her "preaching." Occasionally, something about God slipped out of Mary, almost as though she couldn't help it, but at least she didn't do it intentionally.

But even in refraining from talking about her newfound religion, Mary exuded something. The old Mary was definitely gone. The edge was harder to see, the mean look softer. She did not speak of Richard Tatum with the sharpness she had before. She was different. Kate wasn't sure she liked the new Mary, but it appeared the new Mary was here to stay.

One early summer day, Kate said she would work inside the cabin while Uncle Ned was outside splitting firewood.

"What? You can drive now. Why wouldn't you go into town?"

"Oh, I don't know. Rosita's gone visiting family in Arizona, and there's nothing I need to buy."

"Aren't you gonna spend time with Mary?"

She kicked up a stone. "No, not today."

He put his hands on his hips. "Don't give up on Mary just 'cause she's all fired up with her God stuff. She's still a good friend. Don't let her bein' religious keep you apart."

"I just want the old Mary back."

"Katy, people change. Sometimes we like the change, sometimes not, but they do change. I kinda like that Jesse guy, even though I never had much use for religious talk."

She groaned inside. Her uncle getting religion would be just too much. The conversation ended and each went to their respective work, Uncle Ned outside and Kate indoors.

As Kate worked, she heard someone call out. Uncle Ned answered. They had very few visitors, not even salesmen, at least not since he'd put the sign up stating their unwelcome status. Kate dried her hands and stepped out the door onto the stoop.

A well-dressed woman approached. Uncle Ned stopped work and edged toward the visitor. Kate held back, but did step off the stoop to the ground.

The woman shook Uncle Ned's hand, and then gave him her card.

He squinted at it. "B. Warrington, Manager of—the power company? We don't have power here, and I sure can't afford to install a line from the road."

"That's just it," the woman said, smiling. "I think I have a mutually beneficial solution."

"Yeah, what's that?" he asked. Kate could tell he was skeptical, looking for the angle. He was just like her, or she was just like him, always trying to figure out what was in it for the other person when they offered you something.

The woman sighed. "I have to explain something first. Please hear me out. I need to tell you who I am."

"Lady, I ain't got all day. I've got lots of firewood to split. It doesn't matter who you are."

The woman stood her ground. "I'm sorry, but it does matter."

Uncle Ned sighed. "Well, spit it out. I got stuff to do."

"You don't remember me, do you—Neddy?"

His mouth fell open. He dropped the ax he had been holding.

His face transformed from confusion to rage in an instant. "Git!"

Kate had never heard him roar with such venom. He pointed toward the road. "Get off my property or I'll—Katy, get my rifle."

Kate stood frozen—he couldn't mean he wanted his rifle to drive this woman away, or could he?

He started to push past Kate, heading, no doubt, to get his rifle.

"Ned, please." The woman stood with hands held out.

Kate grasped her uncle's arm with her soft touch, the one she used to try and calm him. "At least see what she wants," Kate whispered soothingly, low so only he heard. Even though his anger was not directed toward her, she hated seeing him this way. "I'm curious."

He stopped midstride. "Curious about what?"

"What this woman wants and who she is and why you are so angry."

Uncle Ned pulled away and crossed his arms. He looked at the woman, then back at Kate, narrowing his eyes. "Katy, meet Brenda."

"Ohhhh," Kate said. All his anger now made sense.

"I see the girl knows the story," Brenda said sadly. "Anyway, Ned, I came to start making things right between us."

"You will never be able to make things right. You stole my money and my reputation. Everybody in town thinks I'm an abuser. You're just a gold digger."

Brenda held her hands up. "Ned, please. I really meant it when I said I want to make things right. I know I can't take back what I did. I probably can't do much to repair your reputation. But I took out a full page ad in your Pickerel newspaper, stating what I did all those years ago and that you are innocent of all I accused you of. The ad will run next week, all week." She let her hands fall to her sides.

His scowl remained, but he wasn't as tensed up. "You came all the way out here to tell me that?"

"No, as I said before, I am offering a mutually beneficial solution. If you agree, you won't need that generator I hear running."

"It works just fine."

"Yes, but wouldn't you like a freezer, so you could keep your meat in it, instead of smoking it or drying it or whatever it is you do?"

Kate stepped closer to the two adults. "I'd like a freezer, Uncle Ned."

He blew out a long breath. "Go on, Brenda. I'm listening. I still want to know what's in it for you, though."

"I did say mutually beneficial, not to me, exactly, but to my company. If we ran a power line through your property, we'd save distance, and avoid the swampy area where we often have to replace or reinforce poles. We'd need a right of way, legal and all, but not in your way, as far as I can tell. We'd have a pole right—come with me, I'll show you."

"Katy, get my rifle and yours, too."

She obeyed, understanding the potential for harm, especially from hungry grizzlies, maybe not so much from this woman.

After arming themselves, Uncle Ned and Kate followed Brenda along the woods down toward the road. She stopped at a spot between the parking area and the cabin. "We'd leave the main road about where that path runs down to Rainbow Lake, skipping that swampy area between the path and your property. Then we'd put a pole about here and then a couple poles up to the house."

"Brenda, I don't have money to bring the power up to the cabin. Somebody took all my money."

She ignored his jab. "Part of my restitution, paying you back, is I will cover the cost to bring electricity from the pole here the rest of the way to your cabin and pay your electric bill for the coming year.

"The new line will then run across the other side of your property and connect back to the line on the road. The company saves money, plus we'll have fewer power outages, since we won't have to fix the poles in the swamp. We have to replace the whole line anyway, so this saves us poles since it's a straight shot. It would require an occasional truck and linesmen to come on your property any time we need to perform repairs. If you grant us a right of way, we will have that right to do so. We'll also occasionally have to trim some trees to avoid damage to our wires and poles from wind and ice.

"If you agree, the company will draw up a contract for you to sign. I will pay your lawyer fees, also as part of my restitution to you. Just send me the lawyer's invoice and I will take care of it."

Kate motioned to Brenda. "So how about some coffee?"

"I'd love some."

Uncle Ned didn't look overly enthused at having this woman in his home, but he didn't counter Kate's offer.

As they were enjoying their coffee, Uncle Ned asked, "So what's this all about, Brenda? This isn't like you."

"I was hoping you would ask," Brenda said, her countenance brightening.

"I thought money would make me happy, so I *was* a gold digger. After I stole your money, I went on a spending spree, but I found out that wasn't the answer. I was surprised it didn't make me happy.

"So, I thought maybe romance would help. A mutual friend introduced me to a nice guy. We got married. We had an okay life, I guess, but he was killed in a freak car accident. I was so angry—angry at life, at God, at whoever happened to be around."

Brenda leaned forward, her hands folded in front of her. "I was so bitter at my loss, at my plan for my happiness not working, at my husband being taken from me. I had this job that I absolutely should have loved, but I didn't. It paid the bills, but I didn't find what I was looking for."

"Don't tell me," Kate said, shaking her head. "You found religion."

"Religion, no. God, yes," Brenda replied. "Actually, God found me—I didn't find him. I heard someone on the radio say to give my heart to Jesus and he would forgive my sin, heal my heart, and give me eternal life. I realized that was what I had been looking for."

Brenda leaned back against her chair. "I also learned that even though Jesus forgave me, I needed to make amends for the bad things I did to other people, like your uncle here. I am to make restitution for what I took from them. I've been at it for months—it may take the rest of my life, but I wanted to get to you, Ned, before I run out of money and energy."

***

"And that, Dr. Baer, is how electricity came to our little cabin so far off the beaten path," Kate said.

Dr. Baer had a thoughtful look on his face.

"What?"

"God keeps popping up, helping people, making them better," he replied. "Maybe he was, and still is, trying to get your attention."

"Don't go there, Dr. Baer. It's not for me."

"Well, as I understand it, God is for everyone, but not everyone takes advantage of the opportunity to get to know him."

Kate crossed her arms and let her irritation out. "I don't want talk about religion. I'm trying to get rid of my anxiety and nightmares. Those have *nothing* to do with religion. I'd like to focus on the things that are tormenting me."

He nodded. "Of course. I was just making an observation based on your story. But let's definitely focus on what you are here for." He smiled at her. "You are a strong woman. Use that strength to face your fears instead of running from them."

She blew out a long breath. "I don't know if I'll be able to."

143

"I do." His voice was confident. "I've talked with hundreds of people, and I've seen excellent results with those who have the resilience and strength you do."

She stared intently at him, and he seemed to be telling the truth. She could tell when someone was just saying something or when they actually meant it. Did that mean there was hope? She hadn't gotten to the horrible stuff yet, but she had already felt comfortable enough sharing so much of her past. But could she tell him *everything*? And would he be able to help her?

THIRTEEN

"SO, are you ready to delve into hard things?" Dr. Baer asked.

"I don't know if I can go on," she whispered. "The nightmares, the faces, they keep coming at me. Maybe it's because I've been doing so much thinking about them."

"Or maybe it's that you haven't given voice to them. When traumatic events happen to us as children, our perception is often skewed. Things appear larger or more impactful than they really were because our interpretation gives us a faulty view."

Kate crossed her arms. "So you're minimizing the loss of my parents then."

"By no means. I'm not minimizing the pain of that loss, Kate. I was mostly referring to the events we haven't gotten to yet. But let's talk about your parents, now that you brought it up. I know the death of your parents threw you, but it shouldn't be the defining event of your life. It seems like you had a decent childhood and teen years with your uncle. He loved you more tangibly than your parents did, but

you hold this bitterness that life treated you wrong.
You need to bring that event down to its true size."

"Um … I'm not sure what you mean."

"You'd be happier if you chose to let the bitterness go. Yes, it's tragic that you lost your parents.
Yes, grieve the loss—for the rest of your life, if you
must—but let go of the bitterness. It just draws life
out of you and makes you miserable."

She shook her head. "I can't." She looked
away.

"It's time for you to face the truth, Kate. What
happened to your parents was terrible, but it isn't the
end of life. You live like everything is gray. You're
afraid of your own shadow. I see the rings around
your eyes. You look as if you haven't slept in days."

"It isn't my parents' death so much, Dr. Baer.
It's the other … it's the faces." She looked up.

He was tapping his chin with his pen. "Maybe
it's time then. Time to look those terrible faces square
in the eyes, to recount the events surrounding them, to
see what you saw and feel what you felt. Your denial
or refusal to do this hard work is keeping you stuck.
The way to be free is to speak about the horrible
things that happened, and together we can work to
bring them down to legitimate size."

She shook her head vigorously. "Not yet. I
can't. Please, Dr. Baer, please let me give you a little
more background to lead up to them."

He pressed his lips together and studied her.
Then he sat back. "That's fine. As long as we're
headed toward these events."

"Yes." Her body felt like granite. She was almost at the first horror. How could she even speak of
it? But if she didn't say anything and left the office,

the torment would continue. She rubbed her clammy hands together. Sweat beaded her forehead.

Dr. Baer's voice broke into her thoughts. "How about take a deep breath?"

She didn't realize she was holding her breath. Inhaling deeply, she exhaled as much tension as she could.

He smiled. "Okay, so Brenda appeared and changed things. What happened after that?"

She thought for a moment. That part was easy to talk about. She would start slow and stop when she had to. "Things went along normally up to my junior year of high school. We enjoyed regular electricity and bought a freezer. Uncle Ned continued to dry veggies and keep a root cellar, but we did fill the freezer.

"What really bothered me was my uncle's rekindled friendship with Brenda. I actually thought, feared really, that they were going to get married."

***

Kate saw Uncle Ned and Brenda walking over the property long after the electricity had been installed. She realized they were becoming close again. She wondered where that would leave her. In the back of her mind, she knew one day she'd be going off on her own. Didn't Uncle Ned deserve some happiness after all his trouble? But what about now?

One day when she was visiting Rosita, she brought up the subject. "Mama Juanita, I'm afraid Uncle Ned is going to marry Brenda. Three's a crowd, you know."

Mama looked at Kate with compassion in her eyes. "Oh my, Kate! So fragile."

"I am not."

"Ah, but you are," Mama said. "Tough in lots of ways, but still fearful of loss, of losing someone. It makes sense, but loss is part of life. A hard part, but a part nevertheless. It is so much better to embrace the loss, or the potential of loss, than to fight what we cannot change."

Mama dried her hands and motioned for Kate to sit. She grasped Kate's hands. "You could always ask Brenda what her intentions are. I think she would understand your concern. But from what you've said and what I've heard, I don't think she's a threat to either of you. If she did marry your uncle, she'd know you're part of the package."

Kate decided to take the next opportunity to find out. One day Brenda dropped by for a visit when Uncle Ned was out hunting. Kate invited her in for coffee.

Not much for subtlety, Kate went right for it. "Brenda, I'd like to know what your intentions are toward my uncle."

Brenda laughed. "Well, if you think I'm going to marry the old coot—if he ever would ask, I'd have to think hard about it. But I don't think he will."

"Why?"

"Well, Kate, my faith is important to me. I know you hate religious talk, but it is very important to me and I don't think it is to Ned. That would be an issue. Besides, there's so much I did to hurt him. And we've both seen and experienced a great deal in the intervening years. We're different people."

"But you two act like lovebirds. I see you walking, talking, and laughing together. Any time now, I expect to see you two holding hands."

Brenda giggled. "So you're a romantic, are you?"

"I know what I see."

"Well, Miss Romance, anything's possible. But right now, Ned and I are rekindling a friendship. That's all I expect. If we can be friends again, I will be happy. I'll be happy anyway because Jesus is enough, but I'd like to be friends again with Ned."

Later, Kate asked Uncle Ned his viewpoint. He said he couldn't imagine anything more than a friendship with his old flame.

Brenda was a frequent visitor at the cabin, sometimes staying for dinner. As to a budding romance, however, it didn't materialize. They both stated friendship was all they hoped for.

Life went on for Kate. She was becoming a better hunter. She was a quieter stalker and her aim was improving. She did well in school grade-wise. Socially, her knowledge of hunting, tracking, finding her way in the woods, and handling her firearms earned her respect from others, even from most of the boys.

Despite Rosita becoming boy crazy, Kate still occasionally went to her house after school. She kept up her training with Mary who insisted on it. Mary occasionally spoke about God, but not as much as before. Kate was relieved, yet surprised as she overheard Mary speaking on the subject with most of her other clients. Of course, they appeared to be interested, or at least polite enough to listen without arguing like Kate did.

It appeared that things would continue this way until graduation. Kate had begun looking at colleges, contemplating pursuing a business degree. Maybe she would become a high-powered executive like Brenda. Who knew? Anyway, she had to start looking. Maybe things were going to be all right, after all. Of course, she realized that unless there was a scholarship available, she would be limited in her choice of colleges.

In the summer before her junior year, she received a letter from the lawyer overseeing her parents' estate. She found out she would get a sizable inheritance when she turned twenty-one. However, the letter stated she could have monies sent to whatever college she chose.

Kate began devouring college catalogs, searching, analyzing, and consuming information much more enthusiastically as further communications with the lawyer made it clear she could go almost anywhere she wanted as far as money was concerned.

She was happy for the news. She wouldn't have to choose a second-class school, nor make her uncle worry about trying to help her financially.

She still grieved the loss of her parents. She knew she would never get over it. Her bitterness at the world might have softened a little, but it was still burning under the surface.

One day when Kate was training with Mary, she found the moves hard to re-create.

"Again," Mary said. "You're not doing your strengthening exercises, I see."

Kate stopped and stood still with her arms folded. "Come on, Mary. No guy wants a muscle-bound girl to take to prom. I don't understand why you think I need this. Just 'cause you got—" Kate stopped as other clients looked up at them.

Mary put her mouth to Kate's ear. "Just 'cause I got raped. Yeah, it happened to me and, yeah, maybe that's why, but you're going off to college in a year."

"Two years."

"Whatever. We live in a dangerous society. Most guys are nice, especially around here. But you never know, Kate. Maybe you'll need to help someone else who is in trouble, or maybe you will have to defend yourself. Now let's do it again."

Kate had never been so glad to leave Mary's. The girl was nuts—on two counts. Her God—whatever that was—and constantly preparing Kate for being assaulted. When she first told Mary she'd carry a gun, that argument didn't hold up to Mary's self-defense logic. A gun was good, but what if you dropped it or couldn't get to it or it jammed or one of her million reasons to justify hand-to-hand self-defense tactics training.

Kate pushed it from her mind. She knew pretty much everyone, and people watched out for her. She could shoot as well as many of the men in town. She was decent at self-defense. What was there to be concerned about? Nothing. Well, algebra certainly had her worried.

FOURTEEN

KATE had gone to Rosita's for a surprise visit. Receiving no answer to her knock, she let herself into their house with the key she had been given.

"Hello? Anybody home?" Her only answer was silence. She glanced outside and saw both cars were gone, so she knew they were all gone as well. The boys were preteens now with activities of their own, and Rosita was too jumpy after the attack in the woods to stay home alone.

Uncle Ned had dropped her off and left to do errands. It would be some time before he picked her up. She might as well wait to see if they came back.

Kate stood for a few moments wondering what she would do to entertain herself, finally deciding to read a book or magazine lying on the coffee table. Before she could sit down, she heard the kitchen door open quietly. Unusual, Kate thought, as Rosita always called out. She walked toward the kitchen.

Suddenly, a strange man appeared in the doorway between the kitchen and the living room.

Kate's defenses were instantly on alert, her nerves on edge. Her breathing picked up and her heart began to race. "Who are you? Get out."

As if to obey, the man turned back the way he had come, but he suddenly whirled around and raced toward her. After a second of confusion, she fled toward the front door.

The man grabbed her long hair and yanked her backward. Kate hit the floor, her rear landing first, then her hands stopping her. This was what Mary had trained her for. She knew at once this called for a no-holds-barred defense.

Kate braced herself with her hands and swung both her legs horizontally into the legs of her attacker. Caught off guard, the man lost his balance and fell to the floor. He jumped up quickly, but Kate was ready. As soon as he stood up, she gave him a hard, well-aimed kick to his groin. He yelped, bent over, and Kate rushed to the door.

Somehow he edged in between her and the door, grabbing her around the neck with both hands. She swiftly brought both hands up to break his hold, stepped away from him, and kicked him in the shins.

The man drew his fist back and punched Kate hard between the eyes. She saw stars and fought to maintain consciousness. Mary had taught her how to stay awake and continue the fight until victory was achieved. Unable to outmaneuver the man and unequal to his strength, Kate felt herself being pulled to the floor. He slapped her hard across the face as she lay there. She stopped struggling.

"That's better," he said, panting. "Quite a fighter you are, little lady." He threw all of his weight on top of her, pinning her down.

Kate now had little doubt as to what was about to happen. Tears sprang to her eyes. She was going to suffer the same fate Mary had. Instead of giving herself to someone she loved. She closed her eyes in a vain attempt to shut out the horror.

"Now you behave, and then I'll just saunter out of here, got it?"

She heard his zipper open, fear shredding her heart with the sound.

She wanted to pray, but did God even care? First her parents, and now this? Besides, how do you pray to someone who isn't real? Or was he? Would Uncle Ned understand? Would people think she invited the attack?

The man put his lips to Kate's—she jerked away. The man moved swiftly, and suddenly Kate felt a metal blade against her neck. "You do anything, *anything* other than cooperate, I'll slit your throat. Do you understand me?"

Kate nodded slowly.

"Open your eyes," he hissed.

Too scared to resist, she obeyed and looked into the most malicious face she had ever seen. Ice-cold eyes stared into hers. The man grinned, but it was utterly evil. He kissed her hard.

At that moment, the thought came to Kate that maybe he wouldn't let her live after he'd had his fun. Why leave a witness? That actually made more sense. The conversations with Mary about street smarts, about how life works, about evil, all rushed through her head.

He kissed her again. Then leered at her.

Kate tensed her muscles. "Uncle Ned, forgive me."

"What?" the man asked.

Kate boxed both of his ears with her fists, then gouged his eyes with her thumbs, and slid herself out from under him as he howled with pain and rage. She scrambled to get up, shaking all over.

"I warned you," he screamed as he leaped up and lunged for her.

She sidestepped away, but his second attempt at her was successful. She could not escape his powerful grip. He thrust her onto the coffee table, and she slipped to the floor. He kicked at her ribs, but self-defense took over. She grabbed his foot and twisted it as hard as she could, then pulled his foot forward, causing him to lose his balance. He snagged her arm and yanked her to him.

"Now where were we?" He held her in a vice grip and attempted to kiss her again.

Kate turned her head.

He pushed her away, then slapped her viciously across the face. The blow was so hard that she fell to the floor.

He kicked her savagely in the ribs.

Tears sprang to her eyes as she cried out in pain. She was done, and she knew it. Her head swam. It started to go dark. She fought back against the loss of consciousness. Her side hurt so badly. Again, he was on top of her. She could resist no longer. She closed her eyes against the coming horror.

"Open your eyes," he said, pinching her face. She opened them and stared into the awful, twisted grin of unspeakable evil.

Kate lay wide-eyed and whimpering, her body revolting against what was happening. The stress was too much. Try as she might to stay conscious, she passed out.

Suddenly, the door crashed open. Kate groggily regained semiconsciousness.

"What is going on here?" Uncle Ned had arrived.

The man stopped.

She forced her eyes to open a slit.

In a rage, Uncle Ned seized a poker from the fireplace and brought it down on the back of the assailant. The man howled with pain as he was struck again and again.

"Katy, move out of the way."

She could not answer.

Uncle Ned's face was contorted with rage. He roared at the man. "You beast! You killed her!" Again, he slammed the poker on the man's back.

The man yelped. "Stop. You're killing me."

Kate, becoming more alert, tried to keep her eyes open, as they kept trying to close. She tried to speak, but the words would not come.

Uncle Ned smashed the poker down on the man again, then aimed for his head.

Kate finally found her voice. "Uncle Ned, don't kill him."

"Did he—?" Uncle Ned quickly looked at her.

"No, you saved me."

"Can you get up?" His attention was riveted on the man groaning on the floor.

Kate shook her head. "I think he broke my ribs. They hurt like crazy."

The man tried to get up, but Uncle Ned brought the poker down on him again. He roared. "If you move, even a little twitch, next time it'll be your head."

The man lay still.

"Can you get to the phone, Katy? There's one in the kitchen."

"No, I can't get up. Can't you?"

"Katy, I can't leave him."

"I can't get up."

"Well, what're we gonna do?"

Suddenly, the man sprang up, but Uncle Ned jumped back and swung the poker. It caught the man in the back of his head and he fell hard, face-first on the floor.

Uncle Ned stepped quickly around the fallen man, and moved to Kate. He never took his eyes from her assailant but gently lifted her up. He pulled her toward the kitchen and handed her the cordless phone. Then he returned to stand over the man, arm up and ready to strike.

Kate punched in 911. When someone answered, she said, "Pickerel. Ramos home."

"What is the problem?"

"A man is here."

"What man?"

"He ... he ... will you send the police? I near got raped and you're asking dumb questions."

"Are you safe?"

"Yes, my uncle's here, but he's old. Please hurry. He, not my uncle, the man, he tried to attack my uncle. I'm afraid he'll get me."

"Please don't worry, miss. The police are on their way."

The man lifted his head.

Uncle Ned roared again. "I'm still here, you beast. I shoulda beat your head instead o' your back. Put your head down or I'll beat it down. Lift it again and I *will* hit you until you don't move. Got it?"

The man put his head down.

In moments, three policemen swarmed through the door, guns drawn. Two of them cuffed and removed the man, and the third asked if Kate and Uncle Ned were okay. Then a medic and Mary rushed in.

After the medic cleared them, Kate collapsed into Mary's arms. "You saved me, Mary," Kate said, shaking and sobbing. "He almost got me, but he didn't. 'Course, he would've if you hadn't trained me and Uncle Ned hadn't shown up."

"I think God saved you, Kate. I was only an instrument in his hands, as was Ned."

"She just may be right there, Katy girl," Uncle Ned said.

All she could do was cry.

Later on, Kate had an interview with the paper since she was the only victim to survive an assault by known serial rapist Christopher Templeton. He would rape and then murder his victims. Templeton said his threat of slitting their throats if they resisted, combined with his promise of sparing their lives if they cooperated, always made his victims docile. Law enforcement praised Kate and Uncle Ned for stopping this man's reign of terror.

As word spread to other states, Kate received hundreds of letters and emails through the police station, thanking her and proclaiming her a hero. The people in town viewed her and Uncle Ned as heroes. It was awkward and she hated all the attention. It only brought up the horrible memories.

After a while, things calmed down. But Kate was still shaken by the experience. Uncle Ned was still upset as well. They only talked about it once, then just had a silent understanding between them. They both survived—and stopped the beast, and they would always look out for each other. Things were gloomy at the cabin, but they hid it from everyone else.

She stopped by a few times to see Mary, but she couldn't work out. It brought up the trauma. Mary suggested she see a therapist, but Kate insisted she would be okay. Mary always said she was praying for Kate, and Kate thanked her. She knew Mary was showing her how much she cared.

As fall turned into winter, Kate finally began to sleep a little again. But she still couldn't fully relax.

"Hey, check this out, Katy," Uncle Ned said as he sat reading the newspaper after dinner one evening. "Christopher Templeton extradited to Texas to face trial for his crimes there. That boy's in trouble now."

She hurried over to him. "What do you mean?"

"He was in jail here in Montana for attempted assault … for what he tried to do to you. But in Texas, he's wanted for murder. They will likely execute him. Anyway, he's going to be far from here."

After finding out her assailant would be far, far way, Kate thought maybe she could relax. However, she still had nightmares where she would see his face close to hers. She would fight him and try to scream until she woke up, sweating and shaking. She kept telling herself he couldn't hurt her anymore, but the nightmares continued and her soul was tortured.

Kate kept the nightmares to herself. She began to wonder if she were losing her mind. She didn't want to upset Uncle Ned, who often moaned in his sleep. Rosita wasn't safe to talk to, and Mary would

only tell Kate that God was the solution. So she suffered alone, putting up a front that she was over it.

FIFTEEN

"WOW!" Dr. Baer said.

"Wow? That's it?" Kate felt irritation rise up in her.

"I'm overwhelmed by the intensity of what you must have felt." He exhaled loudly and rubbed his forehead. "I mean, to come so close to getting raped and then murdered."

"After all these years, I thought I was over it. But the nightmares have gotten worse ever since I received that letter. I had found a way to cope with the horror by staying busy, driving myself to exhaustion, and then sleeping. The chance of having bad dreams decreased as long as I kept it up."

He leaned forward. "I don't think such a traumatic experience is something you can just 'get over.' It's the same as losing your parents, especially as early as you did. But to be nearly raped, beaten up, and almost murdered by a serial rapist and killer is an experience that will likely never totally leave you, no matter how much time elapses."

Kate stared at the floor a few moments, then raised her head. "So I'm doomed to live forever with nightmares?"

He shook his head. "I didn't mean to imply that. We don't control dreams, at least not directly, but our thought processes can affect them, so what we think about, especially in the few hours before bedtime is important.

"For instance, watching a show about something violent or the news and then going to bed isn't a good idea. Wondering about your assailant definitely wouldn't be good. The second thing will probably be harder, but it will help."

Kate shifted in her seat. "What's that?"

"I'm guessing you never processed your thoughts and feelings about the incident. Sometimes failure to do so causes the trauma to linger more than necessary."

"What do you mean by 'processed'?"

"It means to discover what conclusions you came to due to this event. Put another way, how do you view life in light of this attack?" He paused, putting his hands out. "We can do that now which would make sense since we've come this far."

He drew his hands back and picked up his pen, then tapped it on his notes. "I don't think the nightmares come from the event itself as much as from what conclusions you've drawn from the event. Understanding your conclusions stemming from the event is what I mean by 'processing.' "

She felt her throat go dry. When she was able to speak, her voice came out in a shaky whisper. "How do I keep revisiting this? It's awful, horrible to contemplate."

Dropping his pen, he extended his hands and grasped hers gently. "I don't personally know how horrible it is. What I *do* know is that by speaking about it to a professional for as long as it takes to understand your conclusions, writing in a journal how you felt and thought, and also consciously changing your thoughts about the event, will all help you. These practices reduce the power of fear and helplessness because you will come to see the event in its proper perspective. It's an important event in your life, yes, but it shouldn't be what defines you."

She looked into his kind eyes and sensed genuine compassion from him. He had been caring to her the whole time, and he didn't say she was crazy or give her clichés. She licked her lips. "I don't know if I *can* speak of it anymore. And I certainly don't want to write about it or think about it."

He nodded. "I know it's hard, Kate. It's unfair that it happened. It was horrific and terrible, but addressing it reduces its size and the power it still holds over you. You need to know you are not a terrible person to have had this happen. And it didn't destroy your shot at happiness.

"I'm not minimizing what happened and I'm not saying it wasn't scary or awful. But it doesn't have to be the defining moment of your life, because it isn't. Neither is losing your parents."

He still held her hands. "Are you ready to dive into this?"

She looked around wildly, feeling a tornado of emotions roaring inside of her. She wanted to leap up and run away as far as possible. But he was still holding her hands, grounding her to the present. Doing her best to stop the panic attack, she struggled to breathe deeply. She wasn't in any danger. There was nothing to fear. Plus she had already talked about it out loud and nothing bad happened.

He squeezed her hands a little. "I'm here for you. Take as long as you need."

She nodded. Her heart rate started to slow down and her breathing evened.

Finally he spoke. "Are you ready to look this full in the face?"

Her whole body trembled and her voice nearly failed her. "As ready as I'll ever be."

He let go of her hands, and placed his hand on her forearm. He squeezed gently, then let go. "I want you to close your eyes. I'm right here, and when you get agitated, I will put my hand here again so you know you are safe, all right?"

She nodded and closed her eyes. "Yes, I'll do my best."

He told her to go back, to tell him the story again, but to include her thoughts and feelings, especially the part with her assailant close.

As she hesitantly relayed the story, tears overflowed and ran down her face. After she stumbled her way through to the end, she burst into tears.

Dr. Baer handed her a box of tissues. "I'm proud of you. When you're ready, tell me what thoughts are at the front of your mind."

Sobbing, she whispered whatever came to mind. "I want to be held by and kissed by and made love to by the man I want to spend the rest of my life with, not that terrible man. But … I'm too scared to get close to any man. What if I can't ever get past that?" Fears stabbed her heart relentlessly. She forced them out. "And what if I told someone I loved about the attack, and he didn't want me afterward? Or what if he says I wanted the attention or encouraged it?

How would anyone believe me?" She sniffled. "But the worst part is … is … I fought as hard as I could. But when he pinned me down the second time, I was totally at his mercy. He could have—uh, I'm starting to panic right now."

She stopped. Her heart pounded, her mind raced, and she struggled to breathe.

Dr. Baer squeezed her forearm then released it. "You're safe, Kate. I'm here, I care about you, and I'm listening. Take your time."

Her gaze darted all over the room, always sticking at the door. She wanted to bolt out and never come back. But what good what that do? She'd come this far. What if he could help her? Finally she focused on him. He was calm. Patiently waiting for her. She took a deep breath. "Okay, what now?"

"May I share with you what I think?"

She cringed inside, but forced herself to nod.

"When you shared your responses, I heard you say 'what if' several times. What if he had finished what he began? What if any future boyfriend thinks I encouraged this attack or it was somehow consensual? What if I'm completely helpless again? You probably wonder what if that creep escapes and comes after you. What if? What if?"

He leaned forward. "You're living with a heavy load of what ifs crushing you. Your assailant nearly raped you, yes, but he *didn't*. So that 'what if' isn't valid. What might have happened, didn't. And the majority of people have experienced trauma in their lives—trust me on that—so it's highly likely that a potential mate will care about you, not reject you. Maybe he'll share his story with you first."

Kate blinked. Was that true? She'd been so consumed with herself that she didn't consider that the guys she met might have deep wounds of their own. That certainly was true of Uncle Ned and others she knew back in Pickerel—both male and female. Maybe she *wouldn't* be rejected. That tormenting "what if" might never happen.

Dr. Baer went on. "You're trying to control what you can't. You can't control how a guy is going to react when you tell him about this. Also, you can be as cautious as you possibly can every moment, but you can't control life. You will probably be in situations—different situations—where you feel totally out of control. All of us experience this. I'm sure you have fears that Templeton might escape, but likely he never will. You can be set free from so much torment—and probably your nightmares—if you consciously reject all of the what ifs."

She tried to process what he was telling her. It was true that she lived her life in constant fear. Could she eliminate the many fears that tormented her constantly? It seemed impossible.

"If any of those things ever become a reality, deal with it then. Right now, think about your life at present—what *is*, rather than what *might* be."

He stopped speaking. Silence filled the room as she replayed his words, tears rolling down her cheeks. Would any of his advice help?

When she spoke, her voice was low. "I was powerless to stop him. It was terrible, that feeling to know exactly what horrible thing is about to happen and it's going to happen, and you can't do anything about it. I was helpless."

Her voice gained strength as she continued, tears flowing. "I feel the same way about the nightmares—helpless, like nothing I do will make any difference. Nothing matters. No matter what I do, I am just swept along in events that are going to happen."

"That's an important thing you just said."

"What?"

"You're believing a lie. That lie is that you have no say or control over what happens regarding these nightmares."

She flung her arms up. "You said I can't control things, Dr. Baer. You said that. I wish you'd make up your mind."

He sighed. "Okay, I know it sounds confusing, but it really isn't a contradiction. You can't control events or other people, but you *can* control what you think about. You can change your thinking about this tragedy and reject the what ifs. To do that, you will need to recognize your faulty thinking and take responsibility to change your thought patterns."

His voice, though still gentle, picked up in intensity as he leaned forward. "It will likely feel clunky or unnatural at first, identifying your thoughts and changing them, but it will help and should reduce your disturbing dreams. You can't control things, but you are not helpless either. Don't fall into either trap."

She crumpled tissues in her hands as she thought about what he said. Both points were valid. She couldn't control things, but she wasn't helpless either. And maybe if she stopped thinking fearful thoughts, they couldn't torment her. It was certainly worth a try.

She blew out a breath. "I feel better having spoken about what happened. I don't know if I can do what you've recommended, but I can try. I've never talked about this with anyone, at least not how it made me feel."

"You've taken a major step toward healing." Dr. Baer rubbed his chin and was silent a few seconds. "May I suggest something before you leave?"

"Sure."

"This may be difficult for you to accept, but I want you to just consider it. I do believe that God exists, and I know of countless times when he helped people in desperate situations." He held his hand up. "I can see you're stiffening up, but just give me a moment more."

Kate's body went completely rigid when he mentioned God, and all of her defenses were up. She'd give him thirty seconds, then she was out of there.

"Think about this. Is it coincidental that Uncle Ned came in at just the right moment? I can't help but consider the very real possibility that God intervened, even though you didn't ask him to. Your friend Mary had been praying for you all along, so God could have been answering her prayers."

Kate glared at him. "I have a question for you. If God was real, why did he even let that creep try to rape me?"

"Kate, God doesn't stop all acts of evil. He allows people free will. I do believe God was there with you in that horrific situation. And I do believe he sent Uncle Ned to intervene before you were raped or killed. He even allowed you both to stop a serial killer to save many more lives. That's too much coincidence for me." He shook his head. "My point is that you seem to think you're alone. You have to protect yourself. You have to control everything yourself. And you can't—no one can. But I believe God has been with you all along."

She snagged her purse.

He held a hand out. "You can have tremendous comfort knowing God is with you, even in the midst of unspeakable tragedy. You don't have to go through anything alone. Please remember that."

She was irritated. "Well, you've given me a lot of things to think about today." Then it hit her that he had helped her overcome one of the biggest obstacles she had. Not only had she spoken about that horrifying situation out loud, she allowed her feelings to come out, and he truly cared about what she experienced. He encouraged her and told her she wasn't helpless. She softened her heart and her tone. "Thank you, Dr. Baer. I will consider everything we've talked about today."

"Will you come again? I would love to hear that you've made progress."

"I don't … I will let you know."

***

In a week, she was back at Dr. Baer's office. He greeted her warmly, and she immediately felt safe and welcomed. She'd gone back and forth considering whether to come again, but here she was. Maybe she just missed having someone truly care about her and listen to her struggles.

"How have you been lately?"

She almost started talking about work because it was safe. But that was a waste of time. They both knew why she was here. "I'm trying, but I'm not really succeeding. I still see Templeton's evil face pop up in my mind, no matter how many times I try to push him away. I am careful about what shows I watch, and that's helped. I try hard to stop when I'm thinking of what ifs, and I remind myself that much of life is out of my control."

"That's all very good. Have the nightmares decreased at all?"

"Somewhat." She shivered. "But I still can't get rid of … of his evil look. He haunts me during the daytime, not just at night."

"It will take time. He's controlled your thoughts for so long that it's habit. But you can break that habit."

She looked down, fidgeting with her hands. "I think it's because … there's more I haven't told you." She whispered, "I *want* to tell you. But it's so scary and horrifying."

"More than that man? I can't think what could be worse."

She swallowed hard. "It's too hard to just jump into. Would it be okay to go back where I left off and slowly get to that part?"

Dr. Baer smiled warmly. "Of course. Take your time."

***

After Templeton's assault and his arrest, life seemed to return to normal. Except for Kate. She tried to move on, but the memory stayed fresh. She continued to see that horrific face, to feel his hand on her, to hear the sound of his zipper.

She thought no one could understand. She couldn't share it with her fearful friend Rosita. Mary was into God—Kate didn't want to hear religious talk. Uncle Ned, well, who knew what he thought? He was definitely more protective, making her tell him

170

where she was going and how long she intended to be.

Once when Kate was walking through the center of town, she heard Mary's voice. "Hey, Kate."

Kate groaned, but made her way over. Despite all of Mary's talk about God, Kate owed her. If not for all that training, she would have succumbed much more easily and likely would have become one more victim of Templeton.

"How's my best student?" Mary asked.

She wasn't about to let on how horrible she was doing. "Oh, okay. For your best student, I haven't been around much lately. I'm sorry."

Mary motioned with her hand. "Nobody's inside. C'mon."

They sat in Mary's office. "You're not okay, and we both know it. You had a horrific thing happen to you. I think I understand how—"

Kate jumped to her feet and, pointing her finger at Mary's chest, screamed in her face. "You *don't* understand. Nobody understands. Everybody has gone back to normal, everybody but me. I'll never be okay."

Ashamed of her outburst, ashamed that she attacked the one who'd prepared her for the fight of her life, she dropped down, head in her hands, sobbing her eyes out.

Mary placed a comforting hand on her shoulder.

Kate looked up into the tender face of her friend and mentor. "I'm sorry, Mary. I owe you so much. If it hadn't been for your insistence on training, I'd be raped and dead right now."

When Mary spoke, it was barely above a whisper. "I guess God's not finished with you yet.

Oops! There I go again." She knelt down by Kate's chair. "Kate, I don't mean to say I understand *exactly* how you feel. But I do know the turmoil, the doubts, the questions, the what ifs. I know the pain of feeling helpless, and wondering if I am partially to blame. I know the extreme guilt, even though neither I, nor you, are to blame."

Kate looked into Mary's eyes. They were soft and compassionate—where had tough Mary gone? Yes, Mary knew more than anyone what this was like. Kate could confide in her.

"Rosita's freaked out. She doesn't want me to come over like I used to. Mama Juanita said I'm welcome to come, but when I go over, Rosita stays in her room. She told me to go away when I knocked on her door. I've lost my friend and I didn't *do* anything."

Mary drew her into a warm, gentle embrace. "People are weird in tragedy. I don't get it, but they shun the victims, especially in sexual assault cases. It isn't talked about, so it lies there, festering beneath the surface."

"People don't shun you."

Mary waved her hand around. "How many people do you see in here?"

Kate winced. The place was empty most of the time.

"People look at me differently since I was attacked. I've fought my way back into society. I don't give up when I'm ignored. I come at people, not meanly, but I'm assertive. I do my best to act normal, and sometimes it is just that—an act.

"This isn't something you 'get over.' You never forget it happened. Most everybody else goes back to normal. Well, many people have taken extra precautions since a stranger invaded our town. But for the most part, the event fades from their memory because it didn't happen to them. For us, however, it stays with us for a long time. But you gotta go on living."

Kate folded her arms across her chest. "So how long before you got back to normal?"

Mary shook her head. "You don't go back to what normal was before. Instead, it's a new normal. I wasn't always street smart. I was naive—I didn't have the cold view of the world I have now, although that has been changing by my newfound relationship with … you know who."

Kate was about to tell Mary about her nightmares, but decided she would have to figure it out on her own. She realized Mary still carried her own burden from the attack she suffered years ago, an assault more horrific than Kate's.

"Thank you, Mary. For everything." She bit her lip as tears started to choke her throat.

Mary wrapped her arms around Kate, and then the tears flowed. The two were bonded together more than ever.

Kate went to school, but most often came home right afterward since Rosita avoided her. Even at school, they seldom spoke. It was painful to lose her dear friend, especially now when she really needed all the friends she could get.

What Mary said was true. People treated her differently. It seemed that some kids wanted to approach her, but they seemed too uncomfortable. Unfortunately, they hardly said anything about any subject. It was almost as though she were invisible. She was being shut out for no fault of her own.

The winter of her junior year was the longest she'd ever known. The attack never stopped haunting her. She had gone hunting with Uncle Ned several times, but her heart was not in it. Whenever he gave her a choice, she opted to stay home.

The fun-loving girl who treasured being out in the wilderness roaming around, hunting, snowshoeing, seeing animals, and being out with her uncle was gone. She had withdrawn into herself. She was not rude to him or others, but her soul was too wounded to put forth the effort relationships required.

What Uncle Ned thought of the new Kate, he never said. He seemed to take it in stride.

Spring arrived, breaking winter's hold on the land. But Kate found no pleasure in watching the earth coming back to life.

One evening at dinner, she was staring at her plate mindlessly as usual.

"Hey, Katy."

She looked up.

"I thought we could go for a picnic. The lake is getting pretty, what with flowers beginning to peep out of the ground, you know, to celebrate."

She gave him a moment of eye contact, but when she spoke, her voice was flat. "What are we celebrating?"

Uncle Ned sighed, but returned her gaze. "To celebrate spring, a new year. Katy, I know it's been hard for you, but …"

Kate shoved her chair away from the table and shot to her feet. "You have no idea what I'm going through."

He reached for her hand and lightly grasped her wrist. His eyes glistened. "I know that, Katy, and my heart breaks for you. I've watched you all winter, sufferin' alone. I've wanted to say something, but I didn't know what or how to break through this wall you've built. I desperately want back in, Katy girl."

She pulled her chair back in, reached over to him, and put her arms around his neck. The dam burst, and she bawled her eyes out, her whole upper body convulsing. She felt his rough hands on her shoulders. He heaved with grief as he sobbed along with her.

She whimpered. "I'm sorry. I pushed everyone away. I didn't know what to do or say. Everybody thinks I'm this bad or weird person."

"I don't. You're my Katy girl. Always will be, no matter what. What happened wasn't your fault. It was terrible." Suddenly he growled. "How many times I wished I'd killed that monster."

Kate pulled back from their embrace. She was shocked at the intensity with which her uncle spoke of killing another human being. She knew he had passion and held on to grudges, but to hear him speak that way about her assailant made her realize how much he loved her.

"Well, I'm not crazy about celebrating anything."

"Okay. Maybe another time."

Kate's jaw was set. "No, that's not what I meant. I'm not crazy about the idea, but I have to get back into life. It won't be the old normal, like Mary told me. It'll be a new normal. Let's do a picnic at the lake. It would be nice after being cooped up."

"Saturday, then?"

"Sure."

Despite her sour mood, Kate went all out to make their picnic special. Uncle Ned deserved it, and she did too. She would have an enjoyable time, even though it would take a determined effort.

Saturday afternoon as they left the cabin, she was surprised that he didn't pick up his rifle or shotgun. He always left armed. But she noted with relief that he had his pistol holstered on his hip. Normally, he would have taken both the handgun and either a rifle or shotgun.

"Let's cut through the woods," he said.

"Sure," she replied brightly, acting much happier than she felt. She hoped acting happy would help her feel happy. She was tired of moping around. All around her, the world was happy. The birds sang, the sun shone brightly, buds were covering the trees and bushes.

It was a gorgeous Montana spring day. When they arrived at the lake, Kate gasped at the view. It was stunning, with majestic mountains in the background. She strolled to the lake's edge. A light breeze blew past her and was lost in the trees. The water sparkled with millions of tiny diamonds.

She looked back over her shoulder. "How about right here?"

The wind blew Kate's long brown hair into her eyes and strands ended up in her mouth as she ate. She laughed at the trouble she was having with her hair. It was beginning to feel good to be alive again.

SIXTEEN

"NICE to see you laugh, Katy," Uncle Ned said, as he chewed his sandwich. "Thanks for your food prep."

Kate smiled, then got serious again. Any joy or happiness was fleeting at best.

"You know, Katy, you saved me."

She stopped eating. "Whatever are you talking about?"

He smiled at her. "When you came to me, I was miserable over what Brenda did, over losing Harrison's friendship. I was an outcast in town. I guess you'd call it wallowing in self-pity. Then you came. I had to think about someone else. I had to clean up a bit." He gave her a wink.

Kate smiled, then began to giggle.

"Hey, I didn't smell that bad."

"So you say," she said, remembering her first few days in the cabin. It took a lot of cleaning, washing his sheets, and urging him to bathe more often, even to the point of her telling him she would heat and haul his bath water. She giggled all the more.

"Yeah, well, at least I could cook."

"Tolerable," Kate replied, then laughed till the tears rolled down her cheeks. She laughed so hard she fell over, convulsed in laughter.

He held his hands up in surrender. "Okay, okay. You're a far better cook than I am, much more than tolerable. I wouldn'ta starved, but meals are lots more fun now, that I'll admit."

Kate sat up quickly, the laughter gone. She pointed to the soft ground. Her voice was low. "What's that?"

He peered at the muddy ground where she pointed. She looked into his face. It had immediately gone white. She became alarmed as well.

Uncle Ned quickly stood up and looked over her head to the woods. "Get up slowly."

She obeyed instantly.

"He's back!" he whispered. His forehead glistened.

Kate didn't have to ask. She'd recognized the track in the soft dirt—it was Three Toes.

"I left my rifle in the cabin," he said quietly, his voice quavering, never taking his eyes from looking past her. "I was so happy we were moving past Templeton that I got careless. I guess I figured we were getting a break. The pistol I'm carrying won't likely stop him. I'm sorry, Katy."

She reached out a trembling hand to him.

Despite his terror, his jaw was set. "Well, the mistake's made—we've got to deal with it. We're gonna make a break for it. I see him in the distance, but he's still a few hundred yards off. Now, slowly walk to the woods."

Kate walked slowly, making no sudden moves. Terror made her want to run, but she knew running made predators think you were prey. It was a sheer act of will to only walk.

"When we reach the woods, and are out of his sight, or when he charges, we go as fast as we can," Uncle Ned said.

They reached the woods. "Go, Katy," he hissed.

She ran, completely terrified.

"Faster." Uncle Ned was right on her heels.

Kate heard the snap on Uncle Ned's holster and heard him chamber a round, then heard him snap the holster shut again. He was still panting right behind her.

Suddenly, she heard crashing in the brush behind them. Adrenaline coursed through her veins, propelling her faster than ever before.

They flew for the safety of the cabin. Kate started to look back to see how close he was.

"Don't look back!" Uncle Ned screamed. "Go! Go!"

They raced on—the cabin finally appearing in the distance. Kate wondered how her rubbery legs would make it. Maybe she wouldn't. It was then that she heard the beast's growling.

Kate whimpered, expecting at any moment to be knocked to the ground and ripped to shreds. A terrifying way to die. Tears sprang to her eyes. She had survived Templeton, only to be clawed and chewed to death by this raging beast.

Suddenly she slipped, groaning as she fell to the ground. Uncle Ned fell over her, then scrambled to his feet. He reached for her hand. For a split second, she thought of allowing herself to be attacked so her uncle could be saved. But she reached for his hand. He grasped her wrist and pulled her up.

He pointed to the cabin. "Go. Go." It was in sight, but a furtive glance back told her that the galloping bear was too close for them to make it.

Kate heard Uncle Ned's holster being unsnapped. He clicked off the safety and fired at the charging bear.

"Go! I'll try to slow him, but get to the cabin."

As she raced for the cabin, she glanced behind her.

Her uncle stood and fired repeatedly at Three Toes, who veered away from the bullets coming his way.

Kate fell again, and found herself unable to get up. Uncle Ned grabbed her under her arms, and nearly full-grown as she was, half-carried, half-dragged her the rest of the way to the cabin. He rushed them in, slammed the sturdy door shut, and they both collapsed onto the floor.

Kate gave way to her emotions and bawled her terror out. Uncle Ned put a hand on her to lend comfort. She felt its trembling touch and the sweat of his terror and exertion. She rolled off her stomach to her side to look at him. It was then she noticed that the door was closed and latched, but the reinforcing bar stood by the side of the door.

She grasped his arm and shook it. "Uncle Ned—the bar! If you don't put the bar in place, we're going to be killed." She shook uncontrollably. "Uncle Ned. Please."

He got up and grabbed the bar. When she heard it fall into place, she finally exhaled.

She heard growling, then a scratching sound. "What is that?"

They both stood on shaking, rubbery legs to look out the small window. Three Toes was poking something on the ground.

She took her eyes off him for a moment to look questioningly at her uncle. "What is he doing? He's pawing something, but I can't see what."

Uncle Ned looked, then felt for his pistol. "My gun—that's right. When I turned after shooting at him, my hand hit a tree and knocked the gun to the ground. That's what he's fussing with."

"What ..."

"Apparently he associated either my scent on the handgun or the fact that it made a similar noise with my shooting him years ago," Uncle Ned whispered. "Grizzlies have remarkable memory, a sharp smell, and the ability to reason and associate things."

"You always said a human can't outrun a grizzly," Kate said, her voice shaky. "*We* did."

"Well, adrenaline helped. And, huh," Uncle Ned said, pausing. "Well, I'll be."

"What?"

"The reason we made it is that Three Toes stopped to investigate my gun. Or he was just getting even with it. Either way, there's no doubt in my mind that's why we made it."

Further speculation was not possible, for it was then that Three Toes stared at the cabin.

Kate's heart began beating even more wildly.

Three Toes charged right at them. She leaped back from the window, amazed at his speed. The beast slammed into the cabin door with a force she was sure would smash it in. She shrieked and flung herself into her uncle's arms. Perhaps those who discovered their bodies would know they were together in their final moments.

"The door held, Katy. Look." He pointed.

She saw that the door was intact. Suddenly, there was a crash. The small window they had been looking out of was smashed in. Glass flew under the force of a powerful forearm. Vicious claws reached into the cabin, but she and her uncle had backed out of reach.

Kate looked at Uncle Ned and placed her shaking hand on his arm. It trembled a little, but not as much as hers. "Maybe he'll crush the walls."

He shook his head. "No. The door to the woodshed is shut and barred as well. We can't go out, but we're safe in here. I'm going to call for help."

"I don't know about you, but I'm going up to my room." She strode in that direction. "I'm not so sure about the walls."

"We're safe, Katy. I built this place. I know he can't get in."

She sat on her bed up in the loft, alternating between watching her uncle and getting up to gaze out the loft's window. She saw Three Toes prowl around. He growled, clawed the door and walls, and poked his massive paw into the cabin through the broken window.

"Uncle Ned, come up here, will you? I'm afraid he's going to get in and tear you to shreds."

Although he didn't take her suggestion, she was relieved that he grabbed his rifle. He kept it with him while he used the radio. He turned it on and called the county dispatch. They didn't answer right away, so he called James Harrison while he waited. Although he had calmed down considerably, she noticed a slight tremor in his voice.

"Ned, Ned. Slow down, will ya?" Harrison said. "What's that? A bear?"

"James Harrison, not *a* bear, *the* bear," Uncle Ned replied.

"Are you all right?"

"Scared out of our wits, but not physically harmed, if that's what you mean."

"Kate?"

"She's okay, too."

Okay? I'll never be okay. Not after being assaulted by Templeton and now nearly eaten by a bear. I'll never be okay.

"Ned, I'll be out, but it will take a bit to close the store and get out there," Harrison said.

"No, no, no," Uncle Ned replied. "I'm waiting on county dispatch. Don't even think about coming out here alone. That bear's too tricky for just you and me. Besides, I want to be sure we get him. I want backup."

As soon as he was done with Harrison, county dispatch was calling. "Sorry, Mr. Perkins. Had a multi-car accident. What's up?"

Uncle Ned relayed what had taken place. "Stay inside," the dispatcher said. "We'll get some rangers and volunteers to come help."

Uncle Ned joined Kate up in her bedroom. He hugged her as she broke down.

She wept on his shoulder. "That bear terrifies me."

"I know, Katy. Me too."

"Yes, but even so, you stood and shot at him. Even though you were scared." She hugged him tightly. "You defended me."

"We're safe now. How about coming downstairs? He can't get in." Uncle Ned said, breaking the hug and pulling her arm.

"As long as you don't open the door." She was still trembling, but cautiously followed him down the ladder.

Her heart leaped into her throat when he picked up his rifle and strode toward the door. "Don't open it."

He didn't touch the door, but instead went to the window. He poked the muzzle of his rifle out a little and looked around. Suddenly his rifle was knocked aside and went off, the bullet going wild, missing the bear. He leaped back as a massive paw reached for him. He lost his balance and fell. His rifle clattered to the floor beside him.

She shrieked in terror and backed up. She caught herself and ran to her uncle. She dragged him far from the reaching paw. She crouched low to try to get the rifle without getting clawed. She now understood her uncle's foresight in making the cabin's windows so small. They allowed light and a view, but not entrance for predators.

She held the rifle at the ready, but was shaking so much she doubted she could hit anything. Soon, she saw several armed men walk up to the cabin. Uncle Ned stood shakily. She opened the cabin door. James Harrison was there as well some others. Some wore the uniforms of Montana Fish, Wildlife & Parks wardens.

She and Uncle Ned stepped out on to the stoop. She saw her classmate Larry Kingsley and his father. One of the wardens nodded to Harrison, who walked toward Kate and her uncle.

"Come on," he said. "I'll keep you company while we let the others handle this."

Just before Kate turned to go back in, she saw Jeremy McGinnis, one of her classmates. He appeared to be nervous, not cocky like Larry and his father, but he was there for them. He looked her way, nodded, and waved shyly. Then he was gone with the others.

Kate remembered that courage was doing what one is afraid of. It applied to her and her uncle, as well as to Jeremy. Maybe he wasn't as confident as some of the others, but he was there, doing his part.

Suddenly there was a gunshot. Then another, then several, then many volleys. Then silence reigned once more.

Surely the beast was done for.

Surprisingly, though, the hunters did not return. It was after dark when there was a knock on the door of the cabin. Uncle Ned opened it and one of the wardens stood there.

"Well, did you kill that monster?" Uncle Ned asked happily, as if sure of the answer.

The warden, Cade Forrest, shook his head. "Last anyone saw, he was heading out into the northern wilderness. I don't think anything touched him, although a couple of the boys are adamant that one or two of their rounds found their mark. I don't believe it, not from the way he was running.

"I'm sorry, Mr. Perkins. I know you wanted him dead. What do you call him, something Toes?"

"Three Toes," Uncle Ned replied. "I shot him once, took off two toes, so now he only has three on one foot. He's never forgotten me as the one who shot him, and he'll never rest until he's gotten his revenge."

"With your permission, we're going to set up a spotlight and wait for him to return."

Uncle Ned nodded. James Harrison hung around until late in the evening. At about ten, he stood to his feet. "I'd better go along home. You guys gonna be all right?"

"Yeah," Uncle Ned replied. "Thanks for coming, James. You're a good friend."

Uncle Ned and Kate got ready for bed. He came up to tuck her in, something he had often done when she was young, but hadn't for years. He kissed her head. "Call me if you need me, Katy."

Soon, she heard his snoring. How he could sleep, she had no idea. After what felt like hours, too exhausted to stay awake, she too fell asleep.

SEVENTEEN

KATE slept fitfully for some time, then awoke. She lay in bed wide awake for a long time, but finally fell into a deep sleep.

She found herself fighting for her life. Templeton was chasing her around the cabin. She picked up a handgun, but he knocked it away. He grabbed her roughly and pushed her down to the floor. She kicked and scratched, even biting his cheek. She boxed his ears, kicked his groin. Despite all she did, he never yelped in pain, never stopped coming after her. He knocked her down and again lay on her, smiling that evil grin of his, holding her face so she had to look at him. Then she heard a growl. Templeton jumped off her, laughed at her misfortune, and stepped aside.

Three Toes was upon her. She felt his hot breath as his face was thrust into hers. He opened his mouth to bite her. She turned her head to avoid the inevitable. It was then she saw Uncle Ned. He had been viciously mauled, clawed and bitten, and was lying in a pool of blood. She was soon to experience the same fate.

Kate shrieked in terror. The bear and Templeton disappeared. She sat up in her bed, screaming the whole time. She was drenched in sweat.

Uncle Ned rushed up the ladder.

A few minutes later, a man called from outside. "Are you okay?"

Uncle Ned quickly clambered down the ladder and opened the door. "Just a nightmare," he explained.

"All right," the man replied.

The wardens and a few others stayed for a couple days on a rotation, but there was no sign of Three Toes on any of the watches.

After four days, Cade Forrest came to talk. "We're moving on since a lot of other situations have arisen. I'm having a couple people make a circuit around this property and the lake. That bear makes a very distinctive track, so we'll know if he returns. I'm sorry, but that's the best I can do right now."

The warden strode to the door, then turned again to Uncle Ned and Kate. "Mr. Perkins, I've heard your story and always discounted it as the ravings of a man who was spooked by a bear. But I don't discount it so much any more. I saw the claw marks all over the front of this cabin, and even the ones by the window. That bear really doesn't like you and seems bent on your harm. We will patrol and let you know if we see any sign of his return."

Over the next few days, Kate refused to leave the cabin. Finally, Uncle Ned was able to coax her to walk out on to the stoop. "Katy, I know you've had a couple awful experiences, but—"

Kate cut him off. "I … I can't stand being here," she said softly. "I'm terrified to sleep. Every time I do, I end up seeing their faces. I … I can't live here anymore."

Uncle Ned's face fell. "But this is your home, Katy, our home."

"I'm sorry, I really am. I know you love this place, but it's ruined for me. All the good memories have been replaced by Three Toes's attack. I'm afraid we may not be so lucky next time.

"Just look," she said and gestured toward the front of the cabin. "Do you see what that beast did?"

He looked. "So?"

"I thought about what you said—if Three Toes hadn't stopped to attack your handgun, he would have gotten us. His fury at your gun distracted him. We got lucky."

"Yeah, that did save us. But maybe it wasn't luck."

She stared at him, her arms folded. "What, then?"

"Maybe your friend Mary has something."

"Oh no, not God again," she replied, wagging her finger at him. "There's no way he was involved, even if he does exist. And if he does exist, why did he let Templeton do what he did to me and all those other women? Why did he let Three Toes come after us? And … why did he allow my parents to die? Answer me that."

"I don't know the answers, Katy, but I've seen a change in Mary which she attributes to God. She's still street savvy, but she's kinder. And, as for Brenda, I never in a million years thought she would ever admit, even for a second, that she was wrong. And then to try to pay me back for what she did proves to me that she's a changed woman.

"Can't fault you for being angry, Katy. Such things shouldn't happen. I know you experienced more bad things than any person should. I don't begin to understand how you feel. I'm not saying I do, but ... but it's not good to grow bitter."

"You did."

"You're right, but look where it got me. I hated Harrison for years and lost his friendship for all that time. I couldn't say a kind word to anyone in town. Do you know who was most miserable, though? It wasn't Harrison or someone in town. It was me. My bitterness and my holding on to grudges hurt *me*."

He shrugged and held his hands out palms up. "Katy, I'm not into religion, but I can no longer discount at least the possibility that God saved us. There's not much in the way of logical explanation for Three Toes attacking the gun before coming after us. He was sure of getting us if he hadn't stopped. But he gets sidetracked? I don't think so."

He gently grasped her forearm and made eye contact. "He's smart enough to maybe associate the gun as something similar to what shot him, but what he really wanted is me. I can't get over the possibility that God intervened on our behalf. I can't shake it, even though I want to."

It was too much for Kate—first Mary and now Uncle Ned. She shook her head and went back into the cabin.

They stayed in the cabin for a few more days. School was in session, but Kate stayed home for a week. The thought of facing her classmates after her encounter with Three Toes made her want to run and hide forever. Uncle Ned put his foot down and said she had to go to school on Monday. He just didn't understand.

After her assault by Templeton, she often saw her fellow students whispering to each other while glancing in her direction. Whether it was true that they were talking about her or not didn't matter. She felt like an outcast, or worse, a specimen to be analyzed, not a friend who needed comfort. Life as a student in Pickerel would never be the same. Nevertheless, on Monday, she was back at school.

Kate moved through her days, going through the motions. She did the bare minimum. Life was something to endure, to get through, but not enjoy. It seemed she was trapped in a nightmare, trying to awaken to be released from the horrors, but she could not.

One morning, Kate awoke to the sound of Uncle Ned calling her to get up. When she came down to breakfast, he said, "I have bad news, Katy. Cade Forrest came by while you were still asleep. He said he's going to have to stop the patrolling for Three Toes. It's his professional opinion that Three Toes has left the area. He said he can't spare the manpower with all the other issues going on."

She nodded grimly.

"I'm sorry, Katy."

She sighed. It was no use—she had to tell him. "I can't stay here any longer. Even if the patrols were to continue, I have terrible nightmares. I lie awake as long as possible, just waiting on every little sound, fearing it's him prowling around."

She waved her hand around as she talked. She wiped the sweat off her forehead. "I've even gotten up in the night and shined my flashlight at the door to make sure the bar is in place. I have your old double-barreled shotgun under my bed, loaded, ready to blast him to shreds, with more shells nearby in case I have to reload. Then when I sleep, I see them both—Templeton and Three Toes—out to get me. I have to leave."

"But—"

"I've made up my mind. I don't know where I'm going, but I can't stay here. That's all there is to it."

***

"And that, Dr. Baer, is why I can never go back there. It's why that letter threw me."

He took a deep breath.

"You think I'm wrong, don't you? You think I should read the letter and go visit him, right? Oh, and give in and believe in God too?" She slouched in her seat with her arms folded.

"I'm actually quite moved by your story. I see what you mean about the faces that upset you so much. I think I would've died of a heart attack *before* I reached the cabin."

His eyes seemed to search her face as he paused before continuing. "I'm really careful about telling clients they are wrong. I try to help them think clearly about what happened and assist them in processing their interpretations."

He folded his hands and leaned toward her. "We have more work to do, Kate, but I think you've had enough for today."

Kate, drenched in sweat and totally exhausted, left his office.

The next time they met, Kate asked, "So, Dr. Baer, what's on today's agenda?"

"I was hoping we'd get into the rest of your story up until now. It would help me if I know what happened in between the Three Toes incident and now."

"So you want to know what happened," she said as she thought back.

***

Her determination to leave the cabin never wavered. Uncle Ned continually tried to get her to change her mind. But she couldn't sleep through the night. She was jumpy, nervous. When he stayed awake to guard them from "visitors," her anxiety didn't lessen and her sleep was still fitful. Her only hope was to leave.

Life at school was awful. Her friends mostly avoided her, not knowing what to say about either of the attacks. Both students and teachers would look at her, and then whisper among themselves. It was uncomfortable and awkward for everyone, and it made her feel alone.

As bad as Kate felt at school and as much as life had become a nightmare, the worst thing was the terror of walking from the safety of the cabin out to the truck and back again. Uncle Ned always accompanied her, fully armed in case of any trouble.

Her schoolwork suffered and her grades were falling. She couldn't concentrate. Instead, she daydreamed and kept seeing the face of Templeton, and when she was finally able to send that image away, the vicious, snarling face of Three Toes took its place.

One day at school, Kate felt a touch on her shoulder. She turned to see Jeremy McGinnis looking at her. *That* was odd. Most of her fellow students avoided her, and Jeremy was likely the shyest kid in school, if not in all of Montana.

"What?" She lashed out at a target she could finally identify.

"I ... I'm sorry for all you've been going through, Kate," he mumbled. He then walked away.

Kate stared after him. He was the only one who had even made an attempt to enter her new world. Not even her friend Rosita had said as much as he did. Kate chalked Rosita's lack of comfort up to her jumpiness and fear of what might happen. Since what had happened to Kate with Templeton was in Rosita's own house, that had made her more panicky than previously. As sad as it made Kate feel, she could understand Rosita's lack of engagement.

But Jeremy's attempt to engage her was perplexing. For the quietest kid in school to say what he did was like a whole speech for him. It was as if he sort of understood her pain.

At school one day, Larry Kingsley strode toward her. He had a grin on his face. She groaned. When Larry had a grin like that, it generally meant a "victim" was about to have the honor of being the butt of one of his supposedly funny comments. He stopped right in front of her.

"So, how's it feel to be 'bear bait'?" Larry asked, grinning from ear to ear. "First it was 'wolf bait,' and now it's 'bear bait'!"

Kate fought to keep her tears at bay, but realized she wasn't going to succeed.

Suddenly, Larry was shoved out of her face and knocked to the floor.

"You're such an idiot," someone screamed angrily.

Kate, shocked, recognized Jeremy's voice. She turned to see Jeremy pummeling a prostrate Larry. Larry was viewed as tougher, but he was getting a good beating.

"Can't you see she's hurting?" He screamed into Larry's face, all while continuing to hit him.

"Cut it out, Jeremy," Larry said, struggling to get away. "I was just having some fun. Calm down, will ya? Don't take everything so serious."

Jeremy didn't stop, but continued to hit Larry. A couple teachers ran toward the two boys. One grabbed Jeremy, but he wouldn't stop hitting Larry nor leave the fight. Finally, two other teachers joined in and managed to pull Jeremy off Larry.

Jeremy yanked one arm loose and jabbed his finger at Larry's chest. "You do that again, and I'll really hurt you." He yanked his other arm free and strode away.

Kate, along with the teachers and fellow students, stood open-mouthed at what had just gone down. Quiet, shy, never-make-a-peep Jeremy had not only been in a fight, he had *started* it.

Larry was helped to his feet. His nose was bleeding, but he told the teachers he was okay. Always the tough guy, he had been beaten up by the quiet kid at school. He came over to Kate.

"Guess I had that coming," he said quietly. "Sorry. I shoulda known better than to joke about that. I never had a bear chase me. I probably would have pooped my pants. Anyway, you ought to go see about your boyfriend."

Kate nearly choked. "My what?"

"He obviously likes you. Nobody at school has ever dared take me on, not in the last few years anyway, 'cause they know I'd come out on top," Larry said. "Jeremy didn't even think about that. He just charged right in."

"You're crazy."

"Okay, deny it, but I know I'm right—he likes you."

Every evening Kate and her uncle argued about her leaving. She'd already asked and received Mary's permission to live with her. But Kate had taken the further step of secretly writing the lawyer overseeing her parents' estate to ask him to get her completely out of Montana. She kept everyone in the dark, especially her uncle. She couldn't risk giving him the chance to talk her out of it.

One particular evening, they went at it again. He tried argument after argument to get her to change her mind.

"I want to leave. I want to leave now." She stomped her foot. She'd rarely won arguments with him, but she saw defeat in his eyes.

"I'll help you pack," he said softly.

They climbed the ladder up to her room. He took down the rope holding the blanket that had given her privacy. He then stood by her bed, hands at his side, watching her.

She glanced at him. Big tears welled in his eyes. She held out her hands to his. "I know. It's an awful thing, but I have to do this."

"I know."

He carried a couple of her bags to the ladder and took them down. She glanced around at her much-loved bedroom one last time, trying to remember every detail. Tears rushed to her eyes as memories flooded her mind. She then turned and climbed down the ladder. She surveyed the downstairs of her home, trying to store the images in her brain. She did not expect to return.

She strode out the door, never looking back. The ride into town was very quiet.

Uncle Ned brought Kate's things into the house. He looked at Mary. "I'm sure it's only for a while."

Kate hugged her uncle. "I'm sorry," she said, her tears falling on his shoulder.

"You get better, Katy, then you can come home."

When Kate looked in his eyes, she was almost certain he knew. She wasn't coming back.

Four days later, Uncle Ned stopped by. "A letter from that lawyer came overnight delivery, Katy. Must be something about college?"

She knew he was fishing. She reached out to him, hugging him tightly. Then, while he stood watching, she ripped open the envelope. She read it quickly, then looked up.

She grasped his arm and pulled him outside toward his pickup. She reached for the door and motioned for him to get in on his side.

Once they were both in the pickup, she sighed, then looked at him, tears rolling down her cheeks. She swallowed hard.

His forehead wrinkled and his eyes held worry. "Katy, what is it?"

"I made arrangements with the lawyer to get me out of Montana. This letter says everything is a go."

"What? No, you can't, I mean, what …"

"Please, please try to understand. I *have* to leave. The nightmares are torturing me. I'm going to live near Aunt Sara in my own place. She'll make sure I'm okay. The lawyer is making enough money available for that and other necessities," Kate said through her tears.

He sighed and ran his fingers through his hair. He looked away for a moment, then looked back at her.

She lay her hand on his forearm. "It's a terrible thing, I know, but I have to do this. I love you more than I can say, more than I loved Mom and Daddy even."

He reached out and placed his rough hand over hers. "Well, I did teach you to think for yourself, so there's that. I might have taught you to be resourceful too."

She smiled a little.

"When do you leave?" he asked, his eyes full of tears.

"The lawyer's letter included a bus ticket for tomorrow. I guess that's why he overnighted it. The bus leaves early and I plan to be on it. So this is goodbye."

Tears rolled down his weather-beaten face. "I'll come and see you off tomorrow."

"No, let this be goodbye," she said. "I don't want you blubbering all over me out in public." She gave his forearm a squeeze.

"Yeah, you're probably right," he replied, attempting a smile, then his face sobered. "I'll miss you something terrible, Katy girl."

She looked into his eyes. They were glistening and his face was wet. "I know, and I'm so sorry. I'll miss you something awful, too, but I have to go."

She reached for the door handle.

"Just a minute." He leaned toward her. She leaned toward him, expectant. He kissed her on top of her head. "I'll never forget you, Katy."

Then she left the truck and her uncle. The next day, she left behind the only life she had known since she was eleven years old.

***

"So you just up and left?" Dr. Baer asked.

Kate nodded her head sadly. "That's the last time I saw him. I love that old man, but I just couldn't bring myself to go back. It would be torture for him to come to the city, so we've never laid eyes on each other since that day."

"But you correspond, don't you?"

She shook her head. "That letter was the first contact in a couple years. I gave him my address when I moved here, but we don't write, and he doesn't have a phone, as far as I know."

"Hmmm."

She leaned forward and pointed her finger at him. "I know that 'hmmm.' What are you thinking?"

"Maybe you'd better read that letter."

EIGHTEEN

"SO, Kate," Dr. Baer said as they began their next session, "what happened after you left Montana?"

Now that the traumatic events had been recounted, the rest would be easy. She sighed and smiled. "I had a four-day bus ride. I was in culture shock going from poor cabin life in the wilderness to the bustling city and Aunt Sara's stately old mansion. Compared to Uncle Ned's friendly, warm home, it was sterile and devoid of love, really. Despite my aunt being filthy rich, she seemed unhappy with life.

"There was constant traffic zooming around, tons of people everywhere, and everything was fast-paced. Aunt Sara took me to my apartment, where I lived while I finished high school and went to college. I was alone—again. How I missed the loving atmosphere of my Montana home. Before Templeton and Three Toes, of course."

Her moment of happiness at remembering her childhood home was quickly replaced by her normal sadness. "I learned to be self-sufficient. I didn't have to work other than my schooling since my parents' estate provided well for me. I shopped, cooked, cleaned, all skills Uncle Ned taught me. That part was easy, but I had to learn to cope with being alone."

"But you had friends at school, right?"

"Well, yes. One in high school."

***

Kate gained an unlikely friend in Kellie, who at first was aloof with a chip on her shoulder. But over time, Kate discovered a kindred spirit, as Kellie too had suffered. She lived on the streets on her own after being kicked out of her home by her mother.

Kate would have allowed Kellie to live with her, but doubted she could keep it a secret from Aunt Sara, who looked in on Kate with regularity. She knew her aunt would not allow it.

Kate did, however, allow Kellie to wash her clothes, use the shower, and share many meals at her apartment. Kate was glad for the company, and was happy to share her good fortune. She had enough discretionary money to buy clothes and other necessities for both of them.

Kellie was good for Kate as well. She helped Kate shed some of her country naiveté, which helped her avoid many fax paus, a few of which could have been dangerous. She learned of drug deals, gang wars, and what areas to avoid.

By the time Kate went to college, she was nearly as street savvy as Kellie and would be all right without her mentor and protector. Kellie went to a different college far away.

***

"Sounds like you found a good friend, Kate." Dr. Baer said. "Do you two still communicate?"

Kate shook her head. "I lost track of Kellie after our first year of college. Rosita and I wrote once or twice, but then we sort of moved on, I guess. It's too bad, but that's what seems to happen to me. I lose those I love and who love me."

"Maybe that's not totally true."

"What's that supposed to mean?"

"Well, you have a letter that prompted this whole recounting of your story. Maybe you should actually read it and reply. Your running away hasn't been working. Maybe you need a new strategy, like reading Uncle Ned's letter and responding. Maybe like looking up old friends and renewing contact with them instead of running away."

Tears welled in her eyes, and she could barely whisper the words. "I'm afraid I will lose them."

"Yeah, you might lose them," he replied. "But consider how this fear makes you live such a small, shallow life. You don't hang out with friends, you don't date, and you don't even read the letter from Uncle Ned, who took care of you for all those years. All you do is work yourself to exhaustion and then try to sleep.

"As far as the terrible things that have happened to you, running hasn't eliminated your fears at all. Maybe read the letter and even go back to see Uncle Ned. I think—"

She leaped out of her seat. "Are you crazy? I can't go back there. I doubt Templeton is around, but Three Toes might be. I'd be terrified all over again. No, I'll never go back."

Kate stormed out of his office. Still shaking, she drove to her apartment. Her hands gripped the wheel so tightly her knuckles turned white. Her teeth chattered. Just thinking about going back terrified her.

She was angry—angry at her therapist for suggesting she ought to go back *there*, that she should read the letter. He had no idea how she felt. He hadn't been there, nor gone through what she did. He had no idea what he was asking her to do. None, zero.

After pounding on the steering wheel and venting out loud for a while, she eventually leaned her head back against the seat. She knew the truth. All her protestations, arguments, and hesitations were only putting off what had to be done. It was the only path to wholeness.

She forced herself to open her car's door and mechanically walked the short distance to her apartment. Despite being greeted warmly by a couple neighbors, she spoke to no one. Her eyes were fixed solely on her apartment's door. She fumbled with her keys, grabbed her mail, and went in. She collapsed on the hallway floor, scattering her mail and keys.

She allowed the floodgates to open and bawled her eyes out. When most of her sobbing had subsided, she lay on the tiled floor, too exhausted to move.

Some time later, she awoke, shivering from having lain on the cold tiles. Exhaustion seemed to have seeped into her very bones and deep into her soul. Still she willed herself up to a kneeling position, and collected her keys and mail.

It took every ounce of willpower to make herself stand. She tossed her mail onto the small rolltop desk that held her bills, checkbook, and where her unopened mail generally got plopped.

Her eyes fell on the still-unread letter from Uncle Ned. The letter seemed to beg, "Read me. Read me."

She refused its invitation. Instead, she picked up the day's mail and looked through it. Oh no. Another envelope from him.

She shook her head, trying to put off doing what she knew she had to do. Sighing, she gave in and ripped the envelope open. Another letter. As soon as her eyes fell on the familiar scrawl, tears welled in her eyes. How she missed him. Her fear had kept her from the one she loved so dearly, who loved her more fiercely than her own folks had. Could she ever make it up to him?

She read, "Dear Katy, I hope this finds you well and doing all right. As I heard no reply from my letter of several days ago, I decided to write you again."

Kate felt shame wash over her for her neglect. She read on.

"I have a couple surprises for you, and I'd like you to come back for them. Just give me the word, and I'll send you money for the plane or even get your ticket if you prefer. You'd probably rather I just tell you, but it's so much better in person. Anyway, let me know. I await your reply." It was signed, "Ned Perkins."

Kate dropped the letter on to the desk. She crumpled to the floor, tears now running down her face. Shame mingled with terror. She should call Dr. Baer and ask him. *That's dumb.* She knew what she had to do.

What had Dr. Baer said, something about facing one's fears rather than running from them? Running hadn't worked, so maybe he was right. Just thinking about going back pushed her close to panic. It was as if she were being propelled by some unknown force. Despite her denial, and trying to talk herself out of such a crazy conclusion, she had to go. She was *going* to go.

She sometimes took forever to make decisions about important personal matters. However, when she finally made a decision, she immediately began implementing it. She ordered an airplane ticket, reserved a car, and dashed off a quick reply.

The next day, after mailing her reply to Uncle Ned, she strode into work. She was intent on tying up loose ends and planning the following couple weeks' work for her team. Whether her team could handle things in her absence was another matter.

Kate emailed Dr. Baer to let him know of her plans and to cancel her next appointment. He quickly replied and offered his approval. He encouraged her to be brave.

"This may be the solution to your nightmares," he said. "Your decision to step into your fears, rather than running from them, may reduce their power and maybe even free you from them. Anyway, this trip may bring you some peace and closure. Let me know about it when you come back. Of course, let me know if there's anything I can do while you're away."

She took off the day before she was to leave so she could get ready. She had to pack differently—professional attire would be left home. Warm clothes, roughing-it clothes, would be appropriate in Pickerel. Who knew if Uncle Ned would take her hunting or she would have to clean or gut something? Would she even remember how?

Finally done packing, she began to worry. Her old fears surfaced. What if? What if Templeton got out? Would he come for her? What if Three Toes came around? What if? What if?

She tried to busy herself with fussing around her apartment, cleaning, sorting mail, paying bills, balancing her checkbook—anything to keep her mind from going to bad places.

Try as she might, she could not hold the terrors at bay. Finally, exhausted, she found some respite in sleep.

When she woke up, the terror picked right up where it had left off. She ate a quick breakfast, then showered and dressed. She called a cab and was soon on her way to the airport. She was just busy enough to keep herself from totally freaking out. Thankfully, she didn't have long to wait in the airport and soon was settled on the plane.

A woman with three small children sat next to her. She groaned at the thought of misbehaving kids disturbing her flight. She opened her laptop to check her email, hoping the woman would take the hint and leave her alone.

There was a new email from Dr. Baer. She quickly opened it. "Kate, one more thing I wanted to tell you. I am praying for you, that this visit will bring some healing and closure. I highly recommend it, prayer, I mean. Dr. Baer."

She shut her laptop fiercely, scowling. "The nerve," she muttered.

Wasn't God the one who killed my parents and allowed Templeton to assault me and nearly kill me? Wasn't he the one who let Three Toes terrify me out of my mind? If he cared so much, why did he let all these terrible things happen to me?

Kate's attention was drawn to the woman and her interactions with her children. They were fairly quiet, busying themselves with coloring and looking at books. She wondered how the woman managed it. She watched them the entire flight. It was a sufficient distraction to keep her from dwelling on her fears.

She sat for a few moments in her rental car. *Why do terrible things keep happening to me?*

Something Dr. Baer said popped into her mind. He had challenged her to redirect her thinking. Yes, terrible things had happened to her, but it could have been worse. She could have been raped, but wasn't. She could have been murdered, but wasn't. She could have been mauled by Three Toes, but wasn't.

Then the kicker—he said maybe she should consider that God really is and was looking out for her. Yes, he had allowed some tragedies to occur in her life, but there was good in it too. It wasn't as bad as it could have been.

Kate had argued at the time, but now she considered the possibility. Or maybe she was just lucky. Still, her near misses seemed too consistent to be just blind chance or random luck. She still rebelled at the thought of a caring God, but now it caused less anger, the possibility harder to deny.

Well, if he really is looking out for me, maybe he can make sure Templeton and Three Toes stay far, far away.

Kate arrived in Pickerel sooner than she had expected. Partly because she was early, and partly because she had neglected to keep in contact, she drove to Rosita's home. That place still held a mix of fear and joy, but it was time to let go of the bad feelings and remember the good.

Even before she could close her car door, Kate heard the familiar squeal. "Kate."

Rosita burst out her door and enveloped Kate in her arms. "Your uncle said you were coming."

"Mommy, who is this lady?" a little girl asked, shyly peeking from behind Rosita.

"Mommy?" Kate looked from the girl to Rosita and back.

Rosita nodded. "There's four more too. They're home with Larry."

Kate's jaw dropped. "Not—"

"Yep," Rosita replied. "Larry Kingsley is my husband."

"But he's a hunter … and … trapper and all that non-city stuff you hate. Where do you live?"

"We bought a place about fifteen miles out. He keeps trying to make me into a hunter, but I refuse. He made me learn to clean fish and whatever else he gets, but I'm too scared to go hunting. I refuse to allow him to take the kids either. I've heard too many stories of kids getting shot or shooting someone."

Rosita grabbed Kate's left hand. "No ring, no guy, what's up with that?" She grew serious. "I know why you left and I get it. It was just too much with what happened with that man and Three Toes. I see it in your eyes—you're still not over it."

"No."

Despite her naiveté at times, Rosita understood Kate, sometimes better than Kate did herself. Rosita was not as savvy as Mary, but she did have an emotional intuitiveness and understood Kate.

"Come visit us. Here, I made a map for you. Do you have a cell? Silly me, I'm sure you do. I put my number on the map. I gotta go. I told Larry I'd be late since I was waiting to see you. Give me a call."

Same old chatty Rosita, but Larry? Kate couldn't believe it. And kids, *five* of them.

Kate got back in her car and began the twenty-mile trek to the cabin. As she drove, she marvelled that she had ridden, and then driven these twenty miles so many times to town for school, shopping, laundry, seeing Rosita or Mary. It seemed like nothing then—it was normal. Now, being so unused to the long drive, it bothered her. She did, however, enjoy the scenery. How good it would be to see Uncle Ned. She would beg his forgiveness for neglecting him. Would he be in good health? Suppose what he wanted to tell her was that he was dying? She wouldn't be able to handle it. That was it—he was dying, and he didn't want to tell her in a letter.

Her imagination was running wild again. She stepped on the gas. The suspense was too much, but then she remembered Dr. Baer's frequent admonitions to not live in the what ifs.

A memory came back—she was just coming up a hill, then there was a curve and a favored place for the state police to hide. Several friends had gotten snagged there. She had not, but only due to Uncle Ned's repeated warning. She eased off on the gas, letting the hill slow her back to the appropriate speed. As Kate rolled down the other side, the sunlight hit her eyes, having been reflected off a vehicle hidden back in the trees. She chuckled to herself.

As Kate drew close to home, a huge cloud of dread enveloped her. She had a hundred-yard walk—or run if something were chasing her—up to the cabin from the parking area. What if Three Toes were lurking around? What would she do?

I know. I'll honk the horn and hope Uncle Ned hears me. But when Kate pulled into where the parking spot had been, she discovered something new. There was an actual driveway leading up to the cabin. She drove right up to the porch. She got out, stretched, forgetting who or what might be lurking, but only for a moment, then dashed inside.

"Uncle Ned," she called. There was no answer. She looked around. It was neat, neater than it had been when she'd arrived those many years ago. Maybe her influence had rubbed off on him.

Her eyes fell on a piece of paper on the kitchen table. "Katy, I have to get some items in town. I'll be back soon's I can. I look forward to seeing you. Ned Perkins."

Kate smiled. He always signed his letters or notes that way, not "Uncle Ned," but "Ned Perkins." She opened the door, looked carefully around for any unwanted "visitors" and dashed the few feet to her car. She carried her suitcases into the cabin. She shut the door, then noticing the bar leaning against the wall, picked it up and dropped it into its place, securing the door against her four-legged nemesis or any of his friends.

Kate was home again. She sat down to wait for Uncle Ned's return.

NINETEEN

KATE wondered what was taking Uncle Ned so long. She'd told him she would be here. Yes, she had been early, but not that much. She knew when he went to town, he did what he had to do, then returned home. Maybe he had changed. She smiled as she imagined her quiet Uncle Ned socializing at Harrison's store.

Dark thoughts began to overtake her. Suppose he's been in an accident. Maybe he had a heart attack. She pushed the what ifs away. She told herself that something must have delayed him, but that he would be home soon. After a few minutes, she heard the door latch rattle—he was finally home. Why didn't he come in? She looked at the door. Of course. In her determination to avoid Three Toes, she had dropped the bar into place.

She sprung to the door, removed the bar, and swung the door wide open. She lurched back in horror. There, in all his evil persona, stood her human nemesis—Templeton.

"Hi there, girly. We got unfinished business to attend to."

She stood frozen in shock and fear, but only momentarily. Her training of long ago kicked in. She attempted to slam the door in his face. He was too quick and his foot stopped the door's closing thrust. He entered quickly.

She was nearly overcome with fear and horror. She had fought Templeton off over a decade ago, but then she was young, in shape, and training was fresh in her mind. Would she even remember how to fight? It was then that Mary's coaching words came to mind. "When it's life or death, do whatever to survive."

Still shaking with terror, despite doubting her ability to successfully defend herself, she made the decision to survive. He might get her in the end, but she wouldn't go without fighting with everything she had.

He turned briefly to shut and latch the door. When he turned back to face her, she landed a hard punch right between his eyes. He staggered back. He shook his head and lunged at her. She backed up, then stepped forward and struck at his shin with her foot. He grabbed for her leg, but missed. She landed a blow to his other shin. He cursed and grabbed again—and missed.

She was pleased that she was still quick. Despite her misgivings, her confidence in ultimate victory grew a little.

"No matter, girly. You 'n me have a date." His evil grin hadn't lost any of its terror-inspiring power.

She kept silent, saving her energy for attack, the only thing that might save her. Suddenly, Templeton lunged at her and grabbed her in a bear hug. He squeezed her against himself. She smelled his nasty breath as he pushed his lips against hers. She turned away.

He shoved her back fiercely, then slapped her hard across the face. The blow stunned her momentarily, but again Mary's training kicked in. "Don't lose consciousness, fight it, fight back, strike hard."

Her face smarted, but she swiftly kicked his groin with every bit of force she could muster. He crumpled to the floor, moaning. She whirled, looking for a weapon or means of escape. She spotted the radio and raced to it.

Her trembling fingers fumbled to switch it on, finally succeeding. She pushed the transmit key on the desktop mike. "Mayday! Mayday! Perkins cabin! Need help immed—"

She was punched hard between the shoulder blades and went sprawling to the floor. She was dazed, but she heard the familiar sound of his zipper being opened. She heard a belt hit the floor. That was a new twist. Suddenly he was over her. He deftly flipped her on to her back and lay on top of her.

"Uncle Ned! Help! Help me!"

He put his hand over her mouth. "Oh, girly, Uncle Ned ain't gonna help you none."

She stopped struggling and tried to speak.

"I'll move my hand if you promise not to scream. Nod if you promise."

She nodded, and he removed his hand. She ceased struggling. "What do you mean about Uncle Ned?" she asked, fearing the worst.

He cackled. "If he ain't dead, he's soon gonna be. You see, he's handcuffed to a tree down by the lake and your friend, Mr. Three Toes, is out there, probably chewing on him right now. He's more'n likely near dead. I brought that bear back just for you two. You see, when I'm done with the fun part, you 'n me, we're gonna take a walk down there. I know you been hankerin' to meet Mr. Three Toes face to-face. Now, down to business." He laughed.

Her worst fears had come upon her. Why didn't God help her? Why had he allowed her to come here and face all this? Something else Mary said long ago came to her. "You won't have peace until you surrender to God and invite him into your life." Maybe it was time to consider. Was she to surrender to rape and murder? Is that what God wanted for her? She remembered the peace her troubled friend Mary found all those years ago. Would God help her? Even after she had run from him all her life?

"God, help me," she said.

"God ain't gonna help you now," Templeton said as he lay on her. He pushed his lips against hers.

She swiftly clenched her fists and smashed his ears as hard as she could. She pummeled his temples, then swung her right arm hard against his temple, sliding her body out from under his. He grabbed for her, but she kicked his hand away. He did the same with his other hand, but she kicked it too. She stood up, got her balance just as he lunged at her from a crouching position. She stepped aside and he missed, but he whirled and came at her again.

He got in range and swung his fist at her face.

She stepped back, grasped his arm, and utilizing the force of his swing, pulled him past her. He lost his balance and nearly fell. Before he could turn to face her again, she punched him in the kidneys.

He swung his arm back at her, catching her face in a glancing blow.

Her instincts and training had kicked in. That was to her advantage, but she was older and out of shape as far as hand-to-hand combat went. Her face hurt, her back was throbbing. He faced her again, grinning that evil smile of his. He didn't look very tired, a bit winded maybe, but he looked as though he could go a bit longer. She knew she was close to the end of her ability to resist.

"Wanta keep fighting or just give in to the inevitable, girly? You know, you made it real easy, you comin' up here, but I was gonna come get you. I know where you work and where you live. Once I got out, you were never gonna be safe."

"How about you just leave and we forget this happened?" she said. That way, she'd be safe and could get to Uncle Ned if it were not already too late. "If you keep going, it'll be murder, two counts."

"Girly, I got nothin' to lose. I killed two guards breakin' out, a deputy who recognized me—too late for him, and two fellas who helped me bring Mr. Three Toes up here. What's two more?" He laughed again.

"Now, where were we?" he said, reaching for a nearly exhausted Kate, who stood panting. He again pulled her close.

She looked around, trying to avoid his lips, as well as desperate for any sign of hope, which was quickly fading. Her eyes fell on the ladder built into the wall leading up to her bedroom. It had always been a safe haven for her. Somehow that, or something, or God, gave her the will to fight on.

Her arms hung helplessly at her side. Suddenly, she brought them up between his arms and thrust them outward, breaking his grip. She twisted away and ran to the ladder.

She scrambled up just as she had done as a teenager. She raced across the loft to her bed, and in her panic, sat on it and hugged her pillow. She watched him come up the ladder.

Trembling in her terror, she froze, still hugging her pillow.

"You know you're trapped now, girly? Got you all to myself now with no place to go."

He stopped when he was even with her, with a distance of ten or so feet between them. He arched his back, stretching before getting down to business.

In that moment, she saw an opportunity to go on the offensive. She charged at him in a desperate attempt to send him crashing to the floor below. He clutched her, and they both screamed as they fell off the loft.

TWENTY

THEY landed hard on the kitchen table, Templeton on his back and Kate on top. She was pitched forward. She tucked her head and pushed with her hands to complete the somersault. She leaped to her feet to continue the fight for survival.

He lay across the table, unmoving. She edged closer, Mary's training reminding her that an assailant would fake unconsciousness to lure his victim closer. She wouldn't fall for his tricks.

Keeping her eyes on him, she edged swiftly to the door. She pulled Uncle Ned's handgun from its holster. She checked to ensure it was loaded and slid the action back, putting a bullet into the chamber. All she had to do was flick the safety off and pull the trigger. She kept watching her attacker, but he hadn't moved. She put the holster on and placed the pistol in it.

Now the balance of power had shifted. If he came at her again, she'd put him down. Or ... she could take him out anyway. He deserved it for all the torture he'd put her through, not to mention the others. She could get rid of her fears of him for good.

She removed the pistol from the holster, flicked off the safety, and held it with two hands as she approached him. Her hands shook. She so wanted to put a bullet in his evil face—no, empty the whole magazine into him. She began the pull of the trigger, but then eased off and lowered the weapon. Killing Templeton in such a way would lower her to his level.

She poked him with the gun, but there was no response. She noted his chest rising and falling, so he wasn't dead. She heard a scream from the woods. Uncle Ned was still fighting. She had to get to him quickly, but first she had to secure Templeton.

Rope. She could tie him up. It was then she remembered she had chosen to pay just enough attention to get by during Uncle Ned's knot-tying lessons long ago. She chided herself for paying so little heed to his "you might need to know this someday" mantra, but only for a moment. Time was of the essence—she had to get to her uncle.

She looked around for rope and saw several long pieces hanging on a nail on the cabin's wall. She hastily retrieved several pieces, all while watching Templeton.

Carefully, she nudged him with the gun. He still didn't move. Either he was unconscious or he was a consummate actor. She had to chance it—she tied one end of one strand of rope to his right wrist, then tied the other end to one of the table's legs. She tied his other arm to the other table leg. He would have a hard time getting loose since his hands were separated by several feet.

She did the same with his feet, tying one ankle to another table leg and his other one to the last table leg. He was spread-eagled on the kitchen table. She hadn't done any fancy knot-tying as far as she knew, but he was secured.

Now she needed a weapon to fend off Three Toes and rescue her uncle. His rifle hung in its usual spot, but could she fire and hit the bear in a vital spot, yet miss Uncle Ned? How awful it would be to fatally wound her uncle instead of killing the bear. She couldn't take that chance if there were any other option.

She looked all around the cabin. "God … where are you? I have to save him. What can I do?"

Her eyes fell upon some wood shavings on the floor. Of course. A pine knot torch just might do the trick. Her uncle had often used one to keep predators away when he was out splitting wood.

There were no torches in the cabin, but recalling that he stored them in the woodshed, she ran out there using the connecting doorway. She grabbed the first long one she could reach and raced back inside to ignite it in the woodstove. Remembering her uncle's warning about setting the woods on fire, she looked around and spotted the heavy mittens he used to tend the stove. If she held the torch just right, any burning pitch that fell would land on the mittens instead of her bare hands or the dry woods.

The torch's end was blazing. She removed it from the stove and shut the stove door. Templeton still wasn't moving. She picked up a handful of shavings and went outside, shutting the door behind her. She ran as fast as she could carrying the flaming torch.

As she ran, it hit her that she had to get up close and personal with Three Toes. Despite her terror at such a thought, for her uncle, she would. Yes, even if Three Toes killed her, she had to try. Courage was doing the thing feared.

"God, you got me this far, please let me save Uncle Ned."

She heard another scream, horrible in its terror and intensity. *Please, please, please, let me be in time.*

Despite her doubts of ultimate success, she had chosen to fight back against Templeton. Her efforts no doubt saved not only herself, but who knew how many others? Now she had to take that same fight to the beast who'd haunted her for more than a decade.

Breaking out of the woods into the clearing by the lake, she gasped at the sight of the two enemies engaged in mortal, one-sided combat. Her uncle had blood all over him. Three Toes hit him across the face with a swipe of his powerful, massive paw.

Uncle Ned yelped in pain. "Get away, you monster." His right wrist was handcuffed to the tree, but he tried to raise his left to protect his face.

Her worst nightmares had come to life. However, she had vanquished one of them—with God's help, no doubt. Would he help her again?

"Katy, oh Katy. Run, girl. Get out of here. Where's Templeton?" He screamed as the grizzly bit down on his extended arm.

She was aghast at the blood all over him. She threw the shavings on to Three Toes's hindquarters and held the flaming torch to them. "One down, one to go."

Suddenly, Three Toes yelped. He burst into a dead run toward the lake. She started to plunge the torch into the dirt to extinguish it.

"Katy, don't ... put that out. He may ... be back."

She stuck the sharpened end of the torch into the ground, leaving the burning end upright and blazing. She raced to Uncle Ned and embraced him, blood and all.

"Oh, Katy, how brave you are."

She broke their embrace. "I need to call for help, to get you to a hospital, drive off Three Toes, and arrest Templeton."

"My pocket ... cell ..."

"A what?"

"Yeah ... tower nearby."

Kate whipped out her own phone, saw she had bars, and called 911. Only minutes later, she heard a siren. Uncle Ned's phone began to ring. She retrieved it and answered.

"Kate," James Harrison said. "Where are you? Where's Ned? We heard your mayday call."

"Out by the lake, Mr. Harrison. We need an ambulance. Uncle Ned's hurt bad. And something to cut handcuffs. You better have a gun. Three Toes is around."

Soon a police car and several pickups pulled up. Mr. Harrison stepped out of one of the trucks. Two more police cars roared up. Men broke the handcuffs holding Uncle Ned's arm. A couple kept an eye on Three Toes who had leaped into the lake, extinguishing the fire on his back end. Uncle Ned was laid in someone's pickup and was rushed to meet an ambulance.

After Uncle Ned was whisked away, the police questioned Kate. Mr. Harrison stayed with her. She told them that Templeton had handcuffed Uncle

Ned to the tree and managed to bring Three Toes there.

When Templeton's name was mentioned, Officer Drake, apparently the one in charge, demanded answers. "Where is he? Did you see him? He killed a fellow law enforcement officer. We want him bad. Why didn't he come after you?"

Kate, exhausted, struggled to say any more. Totally drained, she didn't reply immediately.

"Well?" Officer Drake again. "Do you know where he is?"

Kate pointed in the direction of the cabin. "You'll find him in our cabin up there."

Officer Drake and his companions raced to their cars and roared off, sirens screaming and lights flashing.

Mr. Harrison looked at Kate. "Where do you want to go? Maybe Mary's? You could stay there. You'll be safe."

"My car is back at the cabin. I need to go to the hospital to check on Uncle Ned."

Mr. Harrison laid his arm on Kate's. "You're in no shape to drive. Besides, we don't want to get in the officers' way. I'll take you to Mary's, then I'll go to the hospital. Ned'll be in surgery for hours likely. I'll keep you posted."

"All right."

He was talking with Mary as Kate wearily climbed into his pickup. She was exhausted from exertion, terror, and grief. On the bumpy drive, she let herself escape into the blackness of sleep.

TWENTY-ONE

"KATE, wake up." Mary nudged her. "You need to get ready."

She rolled away from Mary and held the pillow over her head. Yesterday's horrific events had utterly drained her, and she was in no way ready to get up.

Mary continued to poke her. "You need to get up. Your uncle—"

"Uncle Ned—is he ...?" She sat bolt upright as she remembered her uncle's frightful condition.

Mary sat on the bed. She reached for Kate's hand. "James Harrison's been there all night. He says Ned's hanging in there. Brenda is coming to take you to the trauma center, so you need to get going."

"Brenda? *The* Brenda?"

"Yeah, her. I have some things to do, plus the gym is open, but I'll be up after closing. Brenda said she wanted to talk with you."

Kate dressed and went to grab a quick breakfast. Mary had set out scrambled eggs, toast, and orange juice for her. Eating quickly, she looked around the dining room. There were a few plaques with sayings on them, more God stuff, but Mary was different. She didn't push her religious ideas. For whatever reason, it was a welcome change.

Kate's eyes fell on Mary's hand. There was a gold band on her left ring finger. She grabbed Mary's hand. "What's this?"

Of all her friends in Montana, Mary would have been the last one Kate would have guessed would end up married.

Mary smiled. "Yeah, I got married. I'm sure that's a shock to you, but what's more shocking is *who* I married. You'll never believe it, not in a million years. I had to do some serious forgiving, but God says to forgive like Jesus forgave me, so I did." She twisted the ring on her finger. "Do you remember Richard Tatum?"

"No, you gotta be kidding me. Didn't he—?"

Mary's smile got broader. It was a full, happy smile. "Well, I never would have considered marrying him since I was so sure he was the one who raped me. I discovered, however, that I don't know everything like I think I do." She winked at Kate.

"Richard served time for the assault on you and Rosita. When he got out, he came to see me, but I was too stubborn to listen to him. Can you believe it?"

Kate nodded. "I can."

Mary shot her a look. "I know. But God worked on my heart enough so I eventually listened after months of Richard trying to talk to me. I was on guard, but I was also drawn to the change in him. The Tatum I-can-do-what-I-want attitude was gone. He found God in prison and faithfully attended Bible studies and services."

Mary folded her hands. "Richard told me who raped me. He didn't come forward back then because he was threatened. He apologized for his complicity and cowardice. He said he was sorry for joining in the attack on you, Rosita, and me. He told me he loved me back when he wanted to date me and loved me still. He said if I could forgive him, he wanted to marry me."

Kate was so engrossed in Mary's tale that she stopped eating. "I hope you turned in the creep who attacked you so he wouldn't hurt someone else."

Mary was silent for a few moments. "We tried, but the guy had witnesses who claimed he was far away when it happened, so nothing came of it.

"I knew Richard hadn't raped me because he had a solid alibi, but he did gang up with his brothers to fight us. So I had a choice—hold onto a grudge against a boy or forgive the new man. I sensed God urging me to give Richard a chance. So I chose to forgive him and let him into my life."

"I don't think I could've done that," Kate said.

Mary nodded. "Only with God, Kate. He makes the impossible, possible. Anyway, I began dating Richard and was intrigued by his desire to follow God as well as his patience. I expected him to kiss me soon after we started dating, but he didn't. He said he'd kiss me when we got married, even though I would have liked it sooner." She smiled impishly. "And his humility—such a change from the Tatum way. He's away on business, but maybe you can come when he's here and see for yourself how he's changed."

"Wow. You, Rosita, Richard Tatum. Who's next?"

"Maybe you," Mary said, her eyes twinkling. "And one more thing, don't you dare think you got away from Templeton on your own. And chasing off Three Toes? Don't take credit for that either," Mary said. "God had your back. He gave you uncommon courage in both instances."

Brenda's arrival rescued Kate from any more God talk. Still, Mary made a good point—it was unlikely Kate could have done what she did all on her own.

Soon, Kate and Brenda were on their way to the trauma center.

"Katy, Neddy wanted to tell you something."

"He said he had some surprises for me, so that's why he invited me up here."

"Yes. You've seen the new driveway, but the more important one he asked me to tell you. He wanted to be the one to share the news, but last night he asked me to do it since he didn't know, um, well, in case he—"

"Yeah, in case he dies." Tears welled in Kate's eyes and rolled down her face. "Let's not go there."

"Don't give up on him."

"I should have gotten to him sooner." She shook her head sadly.

"Stop. You had your hands full with that monster Templeton. I don't think I could've done what you did."

She looked over at Brenda, her eyes searching the woman's face. "Mary says God helped me. I don't know about that, but I don't know how I could have done it, yet I did."

Brenda glanced over at her. "Worth considering, Katy. Do you mind me calling you that?" she asked. "Neddy calls you that all the time."

"It's okay. What did he want you to tell me?"

Brenda grinned. "Well, Neddy asked me to marry him."

Kate involuntarily lurched backward as though she'd been punched in the stomach. Now that she was about to renew her relationship with her uncle, this interloper was getting in the way. She couldn't formulate a reply.

"I know. It's a lot to take in, Katy. He told me he doesn't understand all my 'God stuff' as he called it, but if I still wanted him, he was in."

Kate could hardly find her voice, but when she finally did, it came out as a barely audible squeak. "What did you say?"

"I want to honor my commitment to him from long ago, but things have changed. I'm now a believer in Jesus and I don't know if he is. Now don't glare at me, Katy. I'm not judging Neddy or putting him down. It's just that my relationship with God is the most important thing to me now. I need my husband to share that relationship."

"So if my uncle gets religion, you're gonna marry him?" Her voice was sharp and she folded her arms.

"Katy, you are welcome to your opinion of God and those who believe, but you would be happier if you would be open to him. As to your question, I'm holding off on my answer to your uncle.

"I love Neddy, more than I did before. Maybe I really didn't then, but I do now." She smiled softly, kindly. "But I won't marry him unless he chooses to have a relationship with Jesus. The thought of losing Neddy again breaks my heart, but Jesus comes first."

Brenda suddenly slowed the car, turning on to the shoulder. She put it in park, then turned to face Kate. "Katy, you will never lose the place you hold in your uncle's heart, even if he marries me. He's got a will, and he's leaving the cabin to you, along with the rest of his estate. I have sufficient monies to live on, plus I'm still working. And as to religion, as you call it, if he believes, that will not alter his love for you. He made it clear to me that you're a very important part of the package."

Kate didn't know what to say, so she nodded.

They arrived at the trauma center and asked which room he was in. James Harrison walked over to them. "He's still unconscious in ICU," Mr. Harrison said. "Lots of stitches. He needed a transfusion since he lost so much blood, but don't you worry none, Kate, he's a tough old coot."

Kate tried to hold the tears back, but failed. "Yeah, but he's old now. I finally come back and lose him." She totally broke down, bawling her eyes out.

Mr. Harrison pulled her into a gentle embrace. "Don't give up on him, Kate. You gave him a reason to fight, plus Brenda here, well, er ..."

"She knows, James Harrison, although with a blabbermouth like you around, the whole world is gonna know." She grinned at him.

After he left, Brenda stayed for a while. Then she told Kate she had some work to attend to. She'd be back in a few hours to give Kate a break.

Kate spoke with a nurse who said her uncle was unconscious, but she could go in. She went into ICU and sat down by his bed. She watched him, dozed, doodled on her phone.

"Why don't you step out for some air?" the attending nurse said. "Leave your phone number and I will notify you the moment he wakes up."

Kate walked out into the hallway.

"Hey, Kate," a man's voice said.

She looked up and saw a stranger.

"Sorry, but who are you?"

"Are you serious?" he asked. "Have you been gone so long you forgot everybody? It's Jeremy, Jeremy McGinnis, you know, from school?"

"Oh, yeah, hi, Jeremy. Sorry I didn't recognize you. It's been a while. What are you doing here?"

"I heard you were here. Sorry about your uncle," he said, the words tumbling out like he was nervous. He was talking more than Kate remembered. He had been so quiet in school.

Jeremy grinned. "Word on the street has it that you overpowered that murderer. Any truth to that?"

Kate nodded. "But I really don't want to talk about it." She saw no reason to share her further exploits in driving off Three Toes.

"Works for me," he replied. "Hey, how about we get something to eat?"

She laughed. "Now that sounds like the Jeremy I know. Always hungry."

He grinned.

"But I gotta stay with Uncle Ned or I'd be glad to." Immediately, she noticed his crestfallen face and scolded herself.

He ran his fingers through his hair. "How about I bring something up to you. I … I really want to talk to you."

Glancing back toward her uncle, she said, "All right, I'll go eat with you. The nurse said she'd call me when he wakes up."

Soon they were seated in the trauma center cafeteria. They exchanged small talk and got caught up on what Kate had been up to since leaving Pickerel.

"So what do you do?" she asked.

"I'm a psychologist. I worked with a fellow for a few years, but I opened my own practice in Pickerel a few years back."

He licked his lips. "Kate, I … I don't see a ring. Are you married or is there someone?"

She noticed he had beads of sweat on his forehead. His hands shook.

"Jeremy, whatever is the matter? And, no, I'm quite unattached, probably forever. How about you? Are you married? What is wrong with you?"

He swallowed hard. "I … never told you how I feel. I … I couldn't. I was too scared. I was afraid you'd—"

"I'd what?"

He shook his head and sighed. "I was in love with you and I just couldn't say it and you left before I could tell you. And how could I be married when I was in love with someone else?"

He grasped both of Kate's hands in his, startling her. "Kate, I … it's been a long time. Maybe we're different people, but I'd like to at least try and see if we could, uh, maybe, um, think about …" He looked down at the table.

She swallowed. "What are you asking me, Jeremy?" she asked, stalling, but fearing the answer.

"Oh, whatever, I may as well get it over with," he said. "Kate, maybe we're not right for each other,

but I'd like to see if we are. If we are, then I want to
marry you. There, I said it, and even if you say no, I
said it."

TWENTY-TWO

KATE marveled at Jeremy's bravery. He had rarely spoken up in school, always the sidekick, the wallflower, hating being called on in class. Yet now he had taken a risky chance.

A long-forgotten memory hit her. She recalled the time he had attacked his best friend Larry Kingsley for making fun of her. Larry had seen what she'd missed—Jeremy liked her.

When Kate lived in Pickerel, she imagined herself marrying someone there and living in a cabin like Uncle Ned. She envisioned marrying Larry Kingsley, but he was taken. Rosita had seen to that. But that worked out better. Rosita would enjoy Larry's boisterous personality. But Jeremy? Kate enjoyed quiet, and he was quiet. There might be a possibility here.

"Did that monster—" he began, but didn't finish.

"Rape me?" When he nodded, she asked, "Would that matter?"

He looked alarmed. "Not to me. I just wondered if it would affect you or your answer. Always thinking like a psychologist, I guess." He grinned and hung his head.

"If we are to go on, you might want to drop that habit with me."

He looked up into her eyes. "Duly noted."

"What would it look like, you and me?" she asked, partly to herself.

He shrugged. "I don't know. I know some modern men move for their wife's career, but I don't think I could take the city. Too many people."

She had to smile at his answer. He was quiet and shy, but he was honest. He wanted it to work between them, but he would be true to himself. He was traditional and would want her to move to Pickerel.

"Kate, I have a nice house out in the country. It's more than a cabin and it even has running water," he said, grinning.

"Well, Jeremy, I have a great job."

His face fell. He looked down at the table. "Yeah, I guess I was expecting too much. Well, at least I said what I feel. That's got to mean something." He looked up.

She looked him in the eyes as she leaned forward. Her eyes blazed. "Don't think you're getting rid of me that easily, Jeremy McGinnis." Then, more calmly, she asked, "Are you okay with a wife who works?"

Jeremy shrugged. "Well, yeah, I guess. I mean, I make enough for us both and even some kids."

"If you want kids, then we'd better get at it. I'm not getting any younger."

"Maybe not any younger, but more beautiful."

Kate was about to jump all over him for insincere flattery, but the look on his face stopped her. He looked as though he really meant it.

"Come on, Beautiful. Let's go check on Uncle Ned."

Kate walked, but it seemed her feet were hardly touching the floor. She couldn't believe what was happening.

On the way back to ICU, her phone vibrated. She quickly answered and received the news that Uncle Ned was awake. She and Jeremy rushed back. Since there was no one guarding the door, they both went in.

"Katy," Uncle Ned said weakly, extending his hand. "Hello, Jeremy. Can you give me and Katy a few moments?"

Jeremy nodded and started to leave. "Uncle Ned, I'd like him to stay," Kate said, wanting to include him, to have no secrets between them, especially if they were to be husband and wife.

"Okay, Katy, whatever you want. Did Brenda tell you?"

Kate nodded, "Yes. She said you asked her to marry you. But, Uncle Ned, she wants you to follow religion."

"I know. Maybe that wouldn't be the end of the world. Did that monster Templeton—? Did they get him? How did you get away from him?"

"No, Uncle Ned," she looked at Jeremy too, "Templeton did not rape me. Yes, they got him."

Uncle Ned blew out a breath. "Thank God, I mean, well, that could be accurate. And I can't believe what you did to Three Toes. You were the bravest person I ever did see."

Kate blushed. She was as surprised as he. She had spent the past many years terrified of the faces, then had come face-to-face with both and come out on top.

"Mary says God helped me. I did ask him to."

"Maybe so. Brenda says God spared me to give me another chance for a relationship with him … and with her."

"What did you do to that bear?" Jeremy asked.

"My Katy, a warrior," Uncle Ned said, repeating his praise from many years ago. "She drove that fiend off with a pine knot torch, set his rear end on fire. You shoulda seen it, Jeremy, gutsiest thing I ever did see."

"I had to save you, Uncle Ned," Kate said quietly. "And, Jeremy, this is between us, you understand? I only included you in this conversation, because, um, you know."

"It'll be our secret. Say, Kate, I have to go. I have an appointment, but I want to see you later. Here's my number," he said, handing her his card.

After Jeremy left, Uncle Ned said, "Did he ask you?"

"Ask me what?"

"Well, I don't want to spoil it," he replied, his eyes twinkling.

"He talked to *you*?" Kate asked. "Why?"

"Because he's very polite. You know we do things right here in Montana," Uncle Ned replied.

"Yeah, he asked me to think about it. I don't know how it would work, honestly, Uncle Ned. He wants kids, and I'm not young anymore."

"Yeah, you're over the hill, girl," Uncle Ned said, half-smiling.

"Well, that's why I asked him to stay. If we're going to be married, I don't want secrets. Do you think he will tell anybody about what I did to Three Toes?"

"Jeremy McGinnis? Nah, your secret's safe with him. You two would be good for each other."

The nurse came in to check on Uncle Ned and to change his dressings. Kate was asked to leave. He asked her to call Brenda, James Harrison, and Mary.

When Brenda arrived, the nurse was finished, so Brenda went in. Kate held back to give them time together, but she did watch. After kissing Uncle Ned's cheek, Brenda sat holding his hand. Kate realized she could not stand in the way of her uncle's relationship with Brenda. After all this time, he deserved some happiness. He seemed agreeable to Brenda's requirement, so he might be going to church soon.

The pull toward religion or God was happening too fast for Kate's taste. However, it seemed wiser to not resent it, but to be open-minded.

Kate was about to head back to Uncle Ned's bedside when Jeremy showed up. They went in together.

"Hey, Katy," Uncle Ned said. "We could have a double wedding—Brenda and me, you and Jeremy."

Kate was taken off guard and didn't know what to say.

But Jeremy did. "Mr. Perkins, we're very glad for you and Brenda, but Kate and I need some time to reacquaint with each other." He looked at Kate. "That okay with you?"

Relieved, Kate nodded. "You generally know what's best, Jeremy."

"Can I have that in writing for future use?" he asked, grinning broadly. They excused themselves for a few moments alone.

"Do you really want to do this—us, I mean, Jeremy?" Kate asked, the old uncertainties threatening to overcome her and steal any hope for happiness.

He held her by the shoulders, and looked deeply into her eyes. "You got away once, Kate. I don't plan to let that happen again. Unless, of course, you want to get away. If that's the case, I won't try to stop you."

She moved toward him, shaking, but still she moved, and rested her head against his chest. He encircled her with his arms and kissed the top of her head.

TWENTY-THREE

KATE had planned to spend a week or so in Montana. However, an alarming email from her secretary made her decide to go back early. The situation with Five had come to a head in her absence.

She made an appointment with Dr. Baer to get him caught up with all that went on in Montana so she could concentrate on the problems at work. After recounting all that occurred, she said, "So, Dr. Baer, that's what's been happening since I was here last."

"Wow." He sat in silence a few moments. "I'm … amazed. You defeated the two things you feared, reacquainted yourself with old friends, and found a man who wants to marry you. Are you going to pursue that?"

"Of course. It's not like I get offers all the time, you know."

He ran his hand through his hair. "I had no idea my recommendation to face your fears could have put you in such danger."

"You couldn't have known."

"True, plus I think someone was looking out for you."

She glared at him.

He put up his hands. "Just sayin'."

She sighed. *You know he's got a point.*

"How I got out in one piece, I don't know. But the cool thing is my fear is down to normal levels, I think."

She leaned forward in her seat. "I think what happened is that I faced my greatest fears and survived. I actually approached Three Toes. Do you believe it? I did it to save Uncle Ned, but I confronted what I feared instead of running away. And I defeated Templeton despite my doubts."

"Well, just so you know," he said, a smile creeping over his face, "I did pray for you. It seems God not only delivered you from death, but also from the fears that have held you in bondage."

"Maybe."

"Maybe it's time to let go of your anger at God for taking your folks and for the subsequent traumas you suffered. It will give you a measure of peace plus less emotional baggage to bring to this new relationship."

"It's a lot to take in, Dr. Baer," she said, "but I will consider it."

He smiled kindly, and she remembered the first time he smiled at her with such compassion. "You're making great progress, Kate. We should probably begin considering bringing your therapy to a close."

She put her hands out. "Whoa. Whoa. Whoa. I start making progress and you cut me loose? There's no way I'm ready to quit meeting with you."

He held up his hands. "Okay, okay. Relax, I won't abandon you. Do you remember me saying way back that I never abandon a client? That was true then and it's true still. I'm here for you."

"I'm entering into a relationship with the potential of marriage, which I don't take lightly. You know I haven't had much practice in relationships, so I want you available. Besides, I'm facing some work challenges I need you to help me think through."

"It'll have to wait for next time. I have an urgent appointment."

She bit her lip. "Much as I hate to admit it, maybe some of that praying you do wouldn't hurt."

"I will. You can be sure of it."

"Thank you." She smiled at him before leaving. He had truly helped her when no one else could. And he genuinely cared about her. Finding him wasn't a coincidence, either, was it?

***

When Kate returned to her apartment, she checked her email. There was a lengthy one from Sue, her secretary, explaining what went down while she was away. Before she'd left, she knew Five wasn't up to the work she needed to get done. He either didn't understand it or didn't care. He was too busy throwing his weight around as the boss's son and likely successor. She had hoped her staff could hold it together in her absence. Apparently not.

The email went on to say that Five kept telling her other staff how to do their jobs and that they were doing it all wrong. Two of them had yelled at Five, telling him off and insulting him. Worse, it was done publicly. Four had barged into her department, demanding they apologize, threatening their termination. To top it all off, marketing had just plopped a huge project in their laps with an impossible timeline they had to meet. This was in addition to their regular workload. The last line read, "And one more thing. Four wants to see you the moment you arrive."

That evening, Kate pondered the situation. In the past, she had gone behind Five, doing most of his work for him. Other tasks, mostly supervising, had suffered. It was her normal way, though, to take up the slack of her employees, not just Five. No wonder she was exhausted. Of course, she had done it so she would be too tired to suffer from nightmares. Maybe she didn't need to drive herself so much anymore. Well, other more pressing things had to be dealt with.

What would she say to Four? Could she tell him the truth, could she risk his anger? Hiram Hanson IV had always gotten his way. He was the boss after all. His word was law. She had always given him what he asked—no, demanded.

How did she tell her boss, "Your kid isn't cutting it. He's hurting my whole department. I need to hire someone who can do the work and is a team player. Five isn't the person for the job." Could she get that message across without jeopardizing her own job?

She sighed and sat with her head in her hands. Another decision loomed. Either she maintained the status quo or challenged her boss. It was one of those choices with no great options. However distasteful and risky it was to follow a new path, she couldn't live the old way any longer. Her health was too important, and besides, it wasn't right.

Maybe she was being dramatic, but it seemed to her that if Five were allowed to continue, all her effort to mold her department into a cohesive unit would come to nothing. She didn't have it in her to start over.

Maybe she should just move to Montana, marry Jeremy, and leave all this mess behind. But that wasn't fair to him, nor even to herself. She must not use him as an escape. They had to take it slow, get to know one another, and see if they were compatible.

No, she had to confront Four. As far as she knew, no one had ever challenged or questioned Hiram Hanson IV's right to do what he wanted, even to take advantage of his employees. *Guess it's up to me.*

The next day, as soon as Kate entered Hanson & Son, she saw Four waiting for her. He ushered her into his office and shut the door behind them. Instead of asking about her trip, he got right down to business. He told her two of her staff disrespected Five, and he wanted her to deal with them. If they didn't apologize, terminate them.

She swallowed. What Hiram Hanson IV did not realize was that a new Kate sat in his office. She had faced death, literally, and survived. He didn't pose much of a threat to her. He might terminate her, but that was the worst he could do.

She cleared her throat. For her own sake, for her department's sake, maybe even for the whole company, it was time.

"Mr. Hanson," she said. "Mr. Hanson V—"

"Or, Five, as you all call him," Four said.

"Yes, Five. Mr. Hanson, Five is not up to the task of creating the quality material marketing has come to expect. I have given him ample time and attention."

Although her palms were sweaty, she continued. "Five has not improved at all in the time I've worked with him. I need someone who can work independently, yet cooperates with the other staff. He cannot do either one, plus he interferes with the others, telling them they are doing their jobs wrong. Some of my people have done this work for years. A few of them for longer than Five has been alive. But he acts like their boss."

Despite the scowl on her boss's face, she decided to go for it. "Mr. Hanson, the marketing department just gave me a huge project with a very short time frame. I need every person working together in harmony. Five burned his bridges with my two employees. It's going to take every bit of negotiation I possess to calm them down and get them back to peak efficiency. Plus, I need to hire someone in place of Five—someone who can do the job."

Kate said her piece. Mr. Hanson stared at her, no doubt surprised at her forthrightness, unusual for her. But then, he didn't know she was different. Instead of looking down, she gazed steadily into his eyes.

He folded his arms across his chest. "Well, they need to apologize to Five—that's all there is to it," he said. "Either that, or they can leave."

"*They* have to apologize?" Kate asked. "Mr. Hanson, I have no doubt that your son is the one in the wrong here. He's obnoxious and acts like his opinion is the only one that matters. I—"

"Kate, you are way out of line."

"Mr. Hanson, I have always respected you and bent over backwards to meet your expectations. I have driven myself, even to the point where it threatened my health, to accomplish the mission you gave me," she said. Her jaw was set.

"Mr. Hanson, if these two employees are not at their prime creative ability, we will not get the new project done in the time frame marketing set. It is quite unrealistic, but nevertheless, we will try to meet it. Plus, I need to hire someone in Five's place, someone who can create quickly and who gets along with the rest of my staff."

Four exploded. "You will see that they apologize to my son. They will get to work and listen respectfully to his suggestions and implement them. And you—" He stood and jabbed his finger at her. "You will also apologize to him and to me for insubordination, and you will get the work done on time. Now, get out and get to work." He pointed at the door.

Kate walked out, her heart pounding and palms sweaty.

Five was standing by the door. "See you back there." He was grinning from ear to ear.

She walked into her department. Sue, her secretary, met her. "Everyone's gone," Sue said. "They heard Four yelling at you."

"Wait. What? What do you mean, gone?"

"They refuse to work any longer with Five. And unless Four quits yelling at them, they won't be back," Sue replied.

"Well, I can't get the work done with no staff," Kate said.

Sue shrugged. "You gotta stand up to him, Kate. Nobody else will. I'm leaving too. I can't stand it anymore. Good luck." She grabbed her purse and walked out.

Kate, bewildered, stood frozen for a few moments. She then turned on her heels and strode to the marketing department. The manager met her just outside his office door. "Come on in, Kate," he said loudly. "I know we just gave you a big project, but I also know you're up to it."

She refused the proffered seat. "I won't be able to get it done unless Four makes some changes. You'll have to see him."

"Kate, we gotta get this done. We promised some big clients," he said. "Now, be a good girl, and get to work."

She felt the anger rise up inside. She just looked at him. *Be a good girl? What kind of talk was that between professionals?* Anyway, she was done being a "good girl" if that meant getting walked on, yelled at, and taken advantage of.

She shook her head in disgust, then whirled and left his office, returning to her own department. Five waited, grinning broadly. As soon as he saw Kate, he asked, "Where is everybody?" He, no doubt, wanted to gloat that he ended up on top, thanks to dear old dad.

"They're gone, Mr. Hanson, gone until you stop being a jerk," Kate said. "I can't work when I have no staff, so you can tell Dad that our department is closed until further notice."

She picked up her purse, some paperwork, and strode toward the door. "Since you're the last one, you can lock up." With that, she was gone.

She had no idea how things were going to turn out. She might lose her job. That wasn't all right with her, but no one should have to work with impossible standards, expectations, and abuse.

She also didn't know about Jeremy. His was an interesting offer, but it would mean great change. Was she ready for that?

So many changes were facing her—her work, a new-found potential marriage partner, a renewed relationship with Uncle Ned, but those were not all. She had a new consciousness about God. What role had he played? It was hard to deny he had helped her cheat death twice in the past and two more times recently. What did he want with her, from her? What role did he intend on playing in her future, especially with all these changes?

Only time would tell. A lot was up in the air, but one thing was settled—she had a new, different outlook. She would go forth into her future, less afraid, more confident. Her debilitating fears had been dealt a crushing blow, robbed of much of their power to control her. She was free—free to be true to herself and glad to be alive.

ACKNOWLEDGEMENTS

To my Lord Jesus Christ, who has called me to write. It's a responsibility I do not take lightly. You have given me courage to step out in faith with this project. You also led me to people who understand this business. Thank you for always watching out for me!

To my wife, Emma, who helps me behind the scenes in many ways. Emma, you probably don't remember saying this, but you once said something about me being famous as a writer after my death. Your words prompted me to get going, not for the sake of being famous, but to at least write and publish my book. Your words were an important catalyst. Thank you.

To Dr. MaryAnn Diorio, my writing mentor.
MaryAnn, your optimism and encouragement gave me hope that it was possible for me to be a published author. Without your direction, I would still be wondering what my next steps should be. Thank you, my friend.

To Lora Doncea, my editor, who approaches writing with her professional editing glasses on and red pen at the ready. Lora, you and I are going to have to have further deliberations over POV (private joke). In all seriousness, your edits explained where my story wasn't clear, decluttered my overexplaining, put commas where they were supposed to be (and removed them from where they weren't supposed to be), as well as added body language throughout. In short, you're teaching me how to write better. Thank you. I look forward, if God wills, to work with you on future books.

To Rachel Trautmiller, my cover designer and formatter—your cover is awesome! It makes me want to look over *my* shoulder, even though I know what's coming. You made it publisher-ready. Thank you.

To Sheila McIntyre, my proofreader, for helping me get those commas into the right places and still picking up mistakes after we had gone through the manuscript with a fine-toothed comb! Thank you.

To my readers. Thank you for joining me on Kate's Journey of Faith.

ABOUT THE AUTHOR

John D. Strong loves to read stories as well as to tell them. He has written short stories for faith-based publications and wrote several stories for his church's day camp. *Pursuit* is his first book in his series, Kate's Journey of Faith.

John likes to hike and enjoy the beauty of the woods and the mountains. In 2020, he and his wife completed a 17-year quest to become Adirondack 46ers (by hiking all 46 of the Adirondack High Peaks in New York State). Their new challenge is to explore the U.S. state by state.

John teaches an adult Bible class at his church. He believes that God has called him to write, both to entertain and to encourage.

John and his wife live in the house where he grew up, nestled in a small town in the Adirondacks of upstate New York. He is overwhelmed by God's creation in this beautiful spot which provides peaceful surroundings in which to weave his stories.